METEOR

THREE-HEADED MONSTER

J.D. MARTENS

EPIC Escape

An Imprint of EPIC Press
abdopublishing.com

Three-Headed Monster
Meteor: Book #4

Written by J.D. Martens

Copyright © 2018 by Abdo Consulting Group, Inc.

Published by EPIC Press™
PO Box 398166
Minneapolis, MN 55439

All rights reserved.

Printed in the United States of America.

International copyrights reserved in all countries.
No part of this book may be reproduced in any form without
written permission from the publisher. EPIC Press™ is trademark
and logo of Abdo Consulting Group, Inc.

Cover design by Candice Keimig
Images for cover art obtained from iStock
Edited by Amy Waeschle

LIBRARY OF CONGRESS CATALOGING-IN-PUBLICATION DATA
Names: Martens, J.D., author.
Title: Three-headed monster/ by J.D. Martens
Description: Minneapolis, MN : EPIC Press, 2018 | Series: The Meteor; #4
Summary: After the comet's fracture, the world braces for one of the fragments to land
    somewhere on the Eurasian Plate. While humanity struggles to survive under these new
    onerous circumstances, Robert and his team must find a way—with limited resources—to
    stop the other comet fragments from hitting Earth.
Identifiers: LCCN 2017946138 | ISBN 9781680768305 (lib. bdg.)
    | ISBN 9781680768589 (ebook)
Subjects: LCSH: Adventure stories—Fiction. | End of the world—Fiction.
    | Meteor showers—Fiction. | Teenagers—Fiction | Young adult fiction.
Classification: DDC [FIC]—dc23
LC record available at http://lccn.loc.gov/2017946138

For Toos, mijn Moeder,
who gave me more than I ever
could have asked for

1

A NEW DOCTOR, AND ONE REBORN

Almost One Year Later: May 25, 2018
San Antonio Mountain, New Mexico

Suri sat up in her hospital bed. She was incredibly sore and tired, but the retrograde and anterograde amnesia was getting better. Slowly but surely, memories were coming back to her, like pieces in a jigsaw puzzle. Over the previous eight months, she'd returned to her work with Dr. Miller on the comet.

Suri felt very lucky to be alive. It was astounding that she might make a full recovery. The doctors could barely believe it.

She, along with Dr. Miller and the rest of the team, had moved to San Antonio Mountain, ten miles west of Los Alamos, New Mexico. San Antonio Mountain stood as the lone lump in the New Mexico plain, visible from sixty miles away. The facility under San Antonio Mountain was chosen because of its isolation—and because the mountain was volcanic, so it had access to geothermal energy. The United States had, in secret, built a gargantuan nuclear-defense complex under the mountain, and it provided them with the space and security they needed for when the comet hit off the coast of France. Everyone would need to go underground, because the ejecta from the comet impact would heat the atmosphere so much that people living on Earth's surface would likely be cooked alive.

The fragment of the comet was expected to enter Earth's atmosphere in one week. Robert had called it "small." Of course, *small* was relative; it was just much smaller than the one the scientists purposefully fractured. It was still seven kilometers wide, so *small* brought people little solace. The Interplanetary Missiles that had left the Earth before the comet split had all been forced to change direction to hit a different fragment, named simply "Comet 2," which was a staggering twenty kilometers wide. Comet 2 could effectively wipe all life forms off Earth, where as Comet 1 might do only half of that.

At just under four miles in diameter, the impact would blast Western Europe off the map. Robert empathized with the Europeans about this. *It seems like Europe always gets hit with the most violence. You gotta feel for them*, he thought.

Robert's new room was small and even more Armageddon-like than his last. His small, Army-issue twin cot creaked every time he switched sides when he slept. His small desk had one of those green banker's lamps with the brass stand, and a small armoire where he could put his threadbare and rapidly deteriorating clothes. *My rooms keep getting smaller*, Robert thought.

There was a nearly empty bottle of whiskey on his desk. Ever since they moved back to New Mexico, Robert had gone back to drinking. It had been just a little at first, the occasional nightcap before bed, but it slowly turned into a nightly ritual. He even had begun distilling his own swill in his bathroom. After all, Jack Daniels wasn't exactly in business anymore. Dr. Ivanov was helping him, since his family used to brew their own vodka back in Russia.

The complex which the U.S. government and NASA now called home had been built in anticipation of a nuclear world war with the Soviet Union. Both nations had several such underground bunker complexes in the event of a nuclear war, but thankfully none had ever needed to be used—until now. Unsurprisingly, this made the United States and Russia the most equipped to deal with the impending event. Before they moved, Robert had attended a meeting to discuss their choices. He had eagerly listened to President Chaplin and Secretary Brighton evaluating the safest location for their team to move, adding in some information when he thought it was relevant.

"There's Iron Mountain, South Dakota, Cheyenne Mountain Air Force Station, the Denver Airport, the Capitol Building, Camp David, Area 51 . . . "

"We should not be close to water," Robert had remarked. He resisted the urge to ask about Area 51. *If we're all going to die,* he imagined saying, *at least tell me the truth about the aliens.* "The megatsunami that may result from the comet landing in the Atlantic will destroy much of the East Coast shoreline. Hopefully, the land mass of Florida, even with its low elevation, will block the Gulf Coast states and shorelines from the megatsunami. In the event the comet penetrates the Earth's crust, a shockwave may actually create an earthquake on the opposite side of the Earth." Robert's team had calculated this location to be near the coast of New Zealand's South Island.

Brighton and President Chaplin had looked at each other before Chaplin responded, "Agreed, Dr. Miller. We were also going to speak with another team about that."

"What about those other places you just listed off? Will they be abandoned?"

"No, they'll be occupied. Some of the bunkers will be housed by senior officials, and others have been auctioned off to civilians, but they'll all be full," Brighton had answered. In the end, they had decided on San Antonio Mountain as their strategic command center.

• • •

Robert took a quick sip of his vodka and put his memories aside before rushing off to the meeting he was late for.

When Robert arrived to the meeting, Secretary Brighton and President Chaplin nodded for him to sit down. He did so, next to Suri, who was also in attendance, and focused on Dr. Isaac Caldwell, the British scientist who was leading the meeting. Dr. Caldwell was an expert on the Cretaceous-Paleogene extinction—when the asteroid hit the earth and caused the dinosaur extinction. A combined geophysicist and astrobiologist, Dr. Caldwell gave Robert an update on his department's progress.

At first, Robert had been shocked to learn that

there was a department for if the comet actually hit. But Secretary Brighton had calmly mentioned, "You couldn't possibly think we would put all of our eggs in *your* basket, Doctor. We are preparing for all possible futures."

Just like in their complex in the Virgin Islands, they were meeting in the cafeteria of their new bunker. Most of the engineers did their work there—and all of it was underground. Even the Secretary and the President of the United States were living under San Antonio Mountain. Their rooms were of course bigger than the lowly scientists'.

"Of a comet this size and density," Dr. Caldwell began, "the impact will create a crater approximately sixty-one kilometers in diameter on the seafloor—"

"On the *seafloor*?" Robert interrupted, shocked.

"Yes," replied Dr. Caldwell.

"But there are three hundred meters of water at least . . . That means . . . " Robert couldn't finish the thought. Since he'd been so focused on stopping the comet, he hadn't thought of what would happen if it actually crashed into Earth.

"Which means it'll still create that crater despite travelling through around three hundred meters of water, yes." Dr. Caldwell paused as this settled in. "As for the rest of the world, the blast will eject a good amount of rock and debris high into the atmosphere. This debris will be heated, and subsequently the ground temperature on the Earth will be dramatically increased. The heavier objects will fall and essentially destroy anything in their paths. In my expert opinion, the common belief that the Sun will be blocked by debris isn't correct. My findings and experiments suggest that Earth will not be suspended in a kind of winter darkness for years. Instead, I believe the ejecta will return to Earth, transferring much of its kinetic energy to the atmosphere on its way back to land. This will heat the Earth, so everyone will need to go underground.

"There are several converted bomb shelters—like the one we are in now. They are also equipped with massive batteries, and we have run wired communication through them. This will only be needed if an electromagnetic pulse, or EMP, is not created. Secondly, there are massive solar panels attached to all of these 'comet shelters,' so after the ejecta from the impact has fallen, some of us will need to exit and clean the panels so that we can convert the Sun's rays into electricity. We've constructed modified space suits to go outside during these initial days after impact. These must be worn because of the intense radiation that may come from the Sun, since the ozone layer may be compromised."

"These are a lot of 'ifs and maybes,' Doctor. Is there a reason so much of this is not certain?" Brighton asked wearily.

"Simple: we have so little historical data. Only a few times has a comet of this magnitude hit Earth. The last time was sixty-five million years ago."

"Ah, okay, well." Secretary Brighton looked warily at his notes before grunting, "Continue, please."

"There is a possibility that the ejecta is light enough

to stay in the atmosphere, which could mean as much as seventy percent of the Sun's light would not reach the Earth's surface. This would mean the end of the world as we know it, because lack of light would cripple all our energy and food sources. But, this is unlikely."

Another member of Dr. Caldwell's team, a man named Dr. Jack Smith, disagreed with a grunt, but said nothing.

"Why is this unlikely?" President Chaplin asked.

"It is unlikely based on the chemical composition of the rock strata off the coast of France, the density of the comet, and our impact modeling software," Dr. Caldwell continued. "The comet will land in a shallow part of the ocean, and because of this we will experience both the effects of a water impact and a land impact."

Secretary Brighton and President Chaplin looked at each other.

"Meanwhile, another devastating event will occur. In the event the comet penetrates the Earth's crust—currently there is a thirty-seven percent chance this will occur—the seismic shockwaves will travel through the Earth and cause earthquakes one hundred and fifty kilometers east of New Zealand. The impact could also catalyze volcanic activity throughout the world. With regard to the United States, the tsunami from the initial impact could affect much of the east and west coasts."

"We've already issued evacuation warnings," Secretary Brighton said.

"Good," replied Dr. Caldwell.

"It is impossible to know for certain, but we speculate that we must spend at least three months underground, using only the modified space suits to venture outside. We estimate that around three billion people will have survived a year after the impact date. This includes the mass fires, widespread earthquakes, aftershocks, volcanic activity, and most importantly, famine. We have also placed large military-grade airtight Humvees at each underground bunker location, complete with temperature-control settings. It's important, though, that for the first month, no one goes outside unless wearing the protective suits I mentioned earlier. Surface temperatures will be well over one thousand degrees Celsius."

The room fell silent.

. . .

Once Dustin and Karina made it on the boat that departed Athens, it took another twenty-four hours for them to reach Izmir, the coastal Turkish city that used to be called Smyrna by the Greeks. Dustin was surprised by how many people had decided to flee Europe so quickly. With the exception of some billionaires (ones who were not currently orbiting Earth in a huge spaceship) who had built their own fortified behemoth complexes in places like the Swiss Alps, everyone was moving south. It was the opposite of the normal path—a sort of comical reversal of the recent wave of immigration. Europe was also much better fitted to send refugees than most nations. Europe had the boats and the infrastructure, and before long, the countries that had previously served as the places to run *from* were now places to run *to*.

Ironically, Syria, Turkey, and Libya were being overrun by the incoming comet refugees. Their governments had tried to protest, and said that they had their own problems, but they quickly capitulated. The refugees fleeing Europe were not welcomed with open arms, since much of the Middle East and northern Africa had fallen into anarchy since the comet became public knowledge. Muslims and Christians alike considered Judgment Day imminent.

By the time that Dustin and Karina had made it to the shores of Izmir, Turkey, borders had all but ceased to exist. Dustin got off the boat with his backpack strapped to his back, which was becoming lighter by the day. They were running out of food.

There was a steady throng of people moving south, and buses were stationed outside, filing people in. Dustin and Karina avoided this line, choosing instead to make a short walk to the U.S. Embassy. It was a beautiful walk and the road was lined with trees. There was no one on the little side street that held the Embassy and they saw the familiar American flag waving above it.

"It's been a while since we've seen that, huh?" Dustin remarked.

"Yeah, reminds me of home," Karina said, reminiscing.

They walked in and showed their passports. The embassy was madly busy. Files were being burned in a trash can in a corner of the office, which Dustin thought was weird because once the comet hit, it seemed like everything would be flattened anyway. They tried to get the attention of someone working, but everyone was moving so fast that his waving and saying, "Excuse me," wasn't really working.

Instead, Dustin stood right in the path of a man carrying an old computer toward the burning trash can, halting his way.

"We are trying to get to Israel, can you help us? We're American citizens," Dustin said firmly.

The man looked thoroughly aggravated. "Yes, yes, and so is everyone else. If you're done, just go down through the back and get in one of the cars. We're leaving in thirty minutes."

"They must think we work at the Consulate," Karina whispered under her voice.

"I just hope that that being a U.S. citizen is enough to have our lives spared," Dustin said. "You don't think they'll ask for proof of employment or anything, do you?"

Karina shrugged. They walked amongst the cacophony, avoiding the Americans running about as best they could as they made their way to the elevator. They got in, took it down to the bottom floor, and composed themselves as they saw seven black SUVs in a line, with their engines running. The front car had the American flags on the front above the headlights.

"That must be for the Ambassador or something," Karina said.

They decided to take the fifth car from the front to be as inconspicuous as possible. They walked up and

Dustin gingerly opened the back side door. There was no one inside. They climbed into the backseat and sat, waiting, holding their passports with sweating palms.

No one questioned Dustin and Karina in the black SUV. It was so hectic with the consulate workers stuffing themselves in, everyone harried and confused, that no one paid them any mind. Dustin and Karina sat with their backpacks on their laps, keeping quiet. The convoy of SUVs left the Embassy, and after a while, Dustin began to relax. Then, the driver and passenger, both Americans working at the consulate in Izmir, spoke to each other, then glanced in Dustin and Karina's direction.

"Are you temps or interns or something?" the passenger asked Dustin. He was a large man with dark glasses and a suit. He looked like a bodyguard.

"Actually," Dustin began, thinking truth would be the best move, "We were traveling, and we're from Houston and thought that Israel would be the safest place to go."

The passenger and driver looked at each other, and then the bodyguard spoke.

"You're not a part of the Embassy?"

"No, we, uh, are American though," Dustin added nervously.

The two suits looked at each other, and then the one who seemed to be in charge shrugged.

"Well, whatever, it's too late now. Kicking you out would kill you at this point. I'm Johnson, that's Wright. I'm from Dallas," the bodyguard named Johnson said, and then pointed to Wright. "He's from Louisville."

"Go Cards," Wright said.

"Go Baylor!" Dustin countered, briefly feeling normal again.

After a long stretch, in which Dustin and Karina both slept, they came to a large road check on the Israeli border.

Dustin asked the bodyguard how Israel held up considering the anarchy everywhere else in the world.

"It almost helped them. They just turned into a

military state, and no one asked them any questions when they kicked all the Palestinians out."

"Isn't that what they already do?" Dustin asked.

Karina punched him in the arm lightly, making a *don't-mess-this-up-with-your-politics* face. Luckily, Wright and Johnson didn't seem to hear—or mind—his comment. Once they made it to the front of the line, they were intensely scrutinized by the Israeli Defense Force. Karina was especially checked, since her dark features may have aroused suspicion in the border guards. Their passports were cleared though, and they were let through.

It took another two and a half hours to get to Tel Aviv, their final location. They did not see much of the city. They drove directly to a very large building and took a right down into a garage. Once they parked, they got out with their backpacks and had their passports checked again. Then they were ferreted down with the two others in their car—Wright and Johnson—into an elevator. It went down five stories. Then, they came out and went even farther downstairs.

"Jesus," Karina said. "We are really heading down into the Earth, aren't we?

Dustin was suddenly too nervous to answer. He was not very comfortable in tight spaces. When he was young he got stuck in an elevator and had a panic attack. Now it was difficult for him to be in them, especially when he was conscious of how much mass was now above him. He briefly considered braving the effects of the comet. Karina held his arm, which comforted him, and they continued down, lower and lower, into the safe chasm. *Breathe in and out, in and out,* Dustin thought to himself.

$\bullet \quad \bullet \quad \bullet$

Jeremy and Anna spent the months before the comet hit planning for their trip to West Virginia, to hide out underground in the caverns of the Lost River. They made preparations, like saving up food from the ration cards, and did everything they could to make sure they would survive. Anna called her parents in Vail and told them to go underground, and they told her they were going to Peters Mountain, West Virginia, where the government had built a massive underground facility. Jeremy's parents were also going there, but when they tried to get Jeremy and Anna on the list, there wasn't any more room.

· · ·

Dr. Nia Rhodes, Astronaut and Captain of Vishnu Spaceship. Day 328:

My name is Nia Rhodes, and I'm an astronaut. The weird thing about this mission is that—for me—it probably won't end well. It is the last mission I will ever do, and I'm here to save the world! It's a tough life, but I've lived a good one. And hey, someone has to do it.

I apologize for any writing errors I might commit. I'm an engineer and a scientist, and the only reason I'm doing this is because the psychiatrist who briefed me before launch said it would help me to make clearer decisions on the mission. I refused to do this for the first 300 days, but now I have seen every episode of How I Met Your Mother, Friends, and Seinfeld at least twice. I gotta find something else to do.

To bring you up to speed: I launched and then headed for Mars, using as little fuel as possible. As I traveled to Mars, NASA's remaining Interplanetary Missiles (IMPs) were sent to Comet 2 to divert its course as much as possible, because once Comet 1 hits Earth, they won't be able to launch any more IMPs, and probably they won't be able to redirect the IMPs either. So they moved Comet 2 as much as possible, and that's where I come in.

Using Mars's gravity, I looped around it like a slingshot, whipping around the planet to gain enough speed to catch up with my target: Comet 2. That was the hard part, and it took a lot of work with Gerald Jan's team on the ground to get it right. But we did it, and now Vishnu (with me inside it) is orbiting around Comet 2, which has a diameter of around forty kilometers.

You want to know something funny? I'm scared of

heights! Terrified. Still, though, I'm at a point now where the word "elevation" no longer has any meaning.

My job is fairly simple: stop Comet 2 from hitting Earth. The impending comet that is about to hit Europe—I can't do anything about that one. At least Gerald Jan has instructed me not to. "Europe will be a casualty," he had told me.

I'm the sole person on Vishnu, Mr. Jan's gigantic satellite. There is a big chance that I won't come back alive from this mission. You know, I bet they'll put up a huge statue of me if Earth isn't destroyed . . .

I'm not actually the only person in space right now, though. After I launched, Gerald told me there was another launch of a gigantic spaceship called the Ark. The Ark orbits Earth, though, and apparently it's the new home of around four hundred billionaires and scientists who actually want the comet to hit Earth. They want it to destroy the billions of people they see as useless so they can begin repopulating the Earth once it returns to equilibrium. I can understand why the billionaires decided to leave Earth, but it's also been revealed that they were connected to the Miami bombing. So not only are they indifferent to the rest of Earth's population, they tried to sabotage NASA. Even for the rich scumbags who did so much to destroy our planet before the comet, it's a new low . . .

I'm in constant contact with the team at Space X right now, making sure that everything is working out on the ship. However, soon, Comet 1 is going to hit the ground really, really hard, and this might cause an EMP (Electromagnetic Pulse for the laypersons reading this). If this happens, things that conduct electricity, like computers and wires and whatnot, will be destroyed. That means no more communication with Los Angeles, and I'm on my own. Uh oh. It's also why Gerald Jan decided to man—or woman in this case—the ship. If an EMP happens, saving Earth will be all up to me. No pressure, right?

So let's hope that doesn't happen. As for the comet itself, it's truly beautiful. I got to see Mars from closer than anyone ever has before. It's been hit by a lot of asteroids and comets, depressions of deeper crimson in *the red planet. The surface is pockmarked like a pubescent teenager's acned face.*

Comet 2 and Comet 3, the two fragments that as of now will hit Earth sometime in December, orbit each other around their center of mass, and I orbit Comet 2. I know this sounds confusing, but since my job is to stop Comet 2, it did not make sense to orbit the center of mass, since it's easiest to hit Comet 2 while only orbiting it.

Anyway, that's it for now. I'll check back. I have to go over some diagnostics, and I get to eat in fifteen minutes. Yay! Space food . . .

2

TIME TO RUN . . . AND HIDE

June 3, 2018, Houston, Texas

The people of China rejoiced when its government told them that the world would not end on June 10th, 2018. So did the people of Brazil, Argentina, and the rest of South America. The elation did not last long, however, because of the intense destruction that would occur. The only country that seemed at peace with everything was Russia. Though they were fairly close in proximity to the blast radius, Russia had been preparing for a nuclear winter for fifty years. They had been certain that the United States would bomb them, and had put in place the Moscow Metro system, a network of tunnels that stretch almost three hundred and fifty kilometers. Since the discovery of the comet, they retrofitted the network to be completely "comet-proof."

Most of the developing world would be untouched by the comet's impact, and there were even some remote tribes living on islands in the Pacific Ocean who wouldn't feel the effects of the comet until it was too late. If somehow the Pacific tsunami did not get them, the heat would.

For those rich enough or lucky enough to find themselves underground with sufficient resources, they would probably survive. As for Jeremy and Anna, they made one quick stop to Major Winter's mansion before heading to West Virginia to go underground.

In a world that was rapidly becoming like those apocalyptic movies he loved to watch as a kid, Jeremy felt like there wasn't anyone better to join them than a Marine they could trust. So he had to see if the major was still there and invite him to go with them to West Virginia.

Robert had told him that he'd have only one day

after the impact to get underground, since that was when the ejecta would reach North America. This would take a total of thirty-six hours to happen, but Jeremy didn't want to take any chances. He drove up to the antebellum mansion and saw Major Winter to the left of his house, holding a gun in his hand. Jeremy got out of the van packed with survival equipment and saw that the major had two men with blindfolds standing against the wall. The major noticed Jeremy out of the corner of his eye, and nodded to him before turning to the two men.

"Any last words?"

But the two men did not respond. They were both dressed in the ragged military clothing that Major Winter also donned. One of them had a cigarette in his mouth. It was a sunny day and sweat formed on Jeremy's brow. Ian Hosmer's execution almost a year before flashed through his mind. The man with the cigarette in his mouth stood straight and erect, while the one to the right slumped back against the wall. He looked a bit like James Dean, only it was hard to tell with the blindfold.

"No? Well, I guess it falls to me. And now—for you—comes the true mystery. Good luck."

And with that, Major Winter's .357 Magnum blasted twice through the air. The two men fell in a slump on top of each other. Jeremy winced. There was a bullet hole through the blindfold of each man. Major Winter was a crack shot.

Jeremy continued staring until Anna came up next to him, shocked.

"Hello, Jeremy. These men, they were not good men." Major Winter sighed heavily, and then looked toward Anna, who had turned white, and said, "I'm sorry you had to see that."

"I just . . . I just wasn't expecting it. That's all," Anna stuttered.

Major Winter and Jeremy stared at the two lumps on the ground, until Major Winter patted Jeremy firmly on the back.

"Well, my boy. How are you? Aside from this whole comet mess, I mean."

Jeremy ignored Major Winter's small talk, and asked, "Major, do you have a place to go underground? I know you've probably heard on the radio that the population needs to go underground for at least three months. Well, Dr. Miller told me that we should head for the Lost River, in West Virginia. It is deep enough and it's near a spring, so we would have fresh water and we've brought enough food to survive. I was wondering if you wanted to come with us."

Major Winter turned serious, furrowing his brow and stroking his beard. He sighed again.

"You are a good man, Jeremy," Major Winter said, stroking his thick black beard. "It's just you and Anna?"

"Yeah, we have enough food for you too if you want to come," Anna responded.

"I have an even better plan," Major Winter responded, turning his head to the big mansion behind him. "You see this mansion? The Thompson

33

family built it. Well, their slaves did. Their slaves were very smart, and when they built the foundation, they built it a full hundred feet deeper than the architect had asked for. They reinforced it, and built a tunnel out of the house, to all the way over there." Major Winter pointed north, far off toward a small river, before continuing, "Unbeknownst to the Thompsons, they were a stop on the underground railroad. If you were a slave on the run in Texas, chances were you spent at least one night at the Thompson Plantation.

"In any event, the tunnels gave them a great head start. The dogs couldn't even chase them. They lost the scent because the tunnels are so extensive and deep. There was no smell to track. In fact, it was my great-great-grandfather who helped design and build this underground network, when he was a slave."

"Wow, Major," Jeremy said, impressed.

"Then, during the height of the Cold War, the owners of this plantation—still in the Thompson family by the way—found out about the network of tunnels. They were also very paranoid about the possibility of a nuclear attack by the Soviet Union, so they decided to make use of what they had found. They reinforced the entire system, putting in rooms, lighting, and huge pantries for food. They were prepared to survive a nuclear winter. The best part was that it was right under their house, and it only needed slight modifications.

"So, back when the Soldiers of God and the Union Anarchists began to take a little control and the reality of the impending comet became too impossible to ignore, I traveled back to where my great-great-grandfather had once lived his remarkable but wretched life as a slave. The plantation was gone, and so was the wealth. Oil companies had bought the surrounding land, and the Thompsons lost a lot of their money in the 2008 financial crisis By the time I got here in 2016, there were only three Thompsons left—three old, decrepit racists. They called me names when I arrived, and told me I was not welcome in 'Master's house.' I killed them, and decided to live in the house that was built on the backs of my kin."

Jeremy looked at the two white men lumped against the plantation's western wall.

"Those men, are they . . . " Jeremy began.

"Misters Austin and Connor Thompson. Brothers, and sons of the men I killed. They returned here a week ago, hoping to reclaim their slave-holding heritage as owners of this building. They killed two of my men before we captured them."

Major Winter looked sadly at the two mounds in the distance, both with wooden crosses sticking out of them.

"Well, what do you say?" Major Winter asked.

"Um, I'm sorry, Major. I don't know what you mean."

"Staying here with me and my men will be a lot easier than driving all the way to West Virginia. Not to mention about a million times safer."

Jeremy considered, slightly taken aback by the major's generosity.

"Do you mind if we have a minute alone, to discuss?" Anna asked.

"Of course, Anna," Major Winter answered. "I'll be inside the house. Just let me know what you decide." Major Winter gruffly straightened out his shirt and walked inside.

"I don't know, Jer, I trust Major Winter, I do, but he's killed six men."

"It seemed like they all deserved it. They were all murderers," Jeremy offered.

"Maybe. What about his men? I've seen the movie *28 Days Later*. Sooner or later the men will go wild for any woman. And if I'm the only one here . . . "

Jeremy had not thought about this, thinking that the danger laid outside, not within. He knew he couldn't protect her from a team of deliriously horny Marines, so he walked back to Major Winter, and declined the offer.

"I'm sorry, Major, but I need to consider the safety of my girlfriend."

The major thought for a second before replying. "I know what you're thinking. Would you come with me for a second? I want to show you something. Then if you still don't want to come, I won't stop you."

The major walked Jeremy over to the front of the house, and Anna looked on in confusion. Jeremy gave her the *give-me-one-second* signal with his finger, and followed behind the major.

They walked into the familiar front room and over to the restaurant. They deposited their guns as usual with the security guard, and Major Winter showed Jeremy the inside of the restaurant. The normally nearly-empty restaurant was almost full of people!

"Twenty men, twenty women," Major Winter said, beaming brightly. "You see, since I opened up this little restaurant in my house, my goal wasn't only to feed people. I was looking for people who I thought would make good people—people who I could save. I figured that a part of the comet would still hit us, and that maybe we would all perish anyway, but it is worth a shot to hide. I'm just trying to save as many people as I can. You won't be alone here with a troop of military men. You'll be in a community. And you'll have to work. We all will."

Jeremy was shocked and incredibly excited. He told Major Winter to wait, and rushed out of the restaurant and through the foyer—accidentally leaving his gun with the security guard.

He told Anna to follow him into the restaurant.

"Jeremy, I'm not hungry. Besides, we should get on the road, right?"

"Just come in, I want to show you something. Then we'll go."

It only took Anna two minutes to make the decision to stay with Major Winter, and they immediately started unpacking the van.

• • •

President Chaplin and Secretary Brighton made calls to all the major government officials of the world. They told everyone to go as far underground as possible, and warned New Zealand that, unfortunately, they were basically screwed. Australia might be shielded from the tsunami by its easterly neighbor New Zealand, but the island nations of Indonesia, the Philippines, Papua New Guinea, and Japan would in all likelihood be swamped by the tsunami. Coupled with the rising temperatures and the other aftereffects of the comet, all Pacific Island inhabitants had no choice but to flee their countries. China's east coast would need to escape as well, but many of the people there had already relocated to bunkers—the ones with connections had, at least.

The West Coast of the United States was evacuated as a precautionary measure, and everyone was made to go inland to an elevation of at least five hundred meters, or fifteen hundred feet, to protect themselves from the likely Pacific tsunami. The Appalachian Mountains made for a nice natural "fence" against the incoming Atlantic megatsunami, so people migrated to its western slopes, and the interior. With the rise in temperature, it was also possible that the polar ice caps would melt by as much as ninety percent before temperatures returned to normal. This would cause a sea level rise of as much as one hundred and fifty feet, effectively swamping all coastal cities.

Ironically, nations that were among the poorest in the world—the Democratic Republic of the Congo, Zimbabwe, and Uganda, for example—were now the most expensive places in the world to get to. People flocked to them as a matter of life and death. Eastern China and the "Stan" countries (Kyrgyzstan, Tajikistan, Uzbekistan, and Kazakhstan) were all relatively safe—as long as its people found a place to wait out the increase in global temperature.

"It's strange," Robert began, listening to President Chaplin call the world leaders, while programming the IMPs to slow the velocity of the smallest comet. The smallest possible velocity was ideal; it would mean less destruction.

"What's that?" Chaplin asked, absentmindedly.

"This is the first time in recorded human civilization when we will go through a true genetic bottleneck. At the very least our population will be decreased by fifty percent. It's strange to know that I'll be one of those that survive, but my daughter . . . "

Robert had not contacted his daughter in over a year, but doubted that she had the resources to get far enough below ground.

President Chaplin stopped what she was doing, and turned kindly toward Robert, putting a hand on his shoulder.

Then she went back to the phone, calling the next country on the list.

"Hello, this is President Chaplin, of the United States of America. Yes, Mr. Prime Minister, I need to tell you . . . "

3

IMPACT

June 10, 2018
San Antonio Mountain, New Mexico

Robert looked at the computer in front of him. It was showing a live feed of a satellite trained on Comet 2, as an IMP bombarded it, changing its orbit ever so slightly away from Earth. Secretary Brighton poked his head into Robert's room.

"Robert, Comet 1 is about to hit Earth, come with me."

Robert nodded, taking his eyes away from his work. *This is the comet we should be worrying about,* Robert thought. *This is the one that might destroy the world.* But he followed Secretary Brighton into a huge situation room where there were several screens showing live feeds of the comet as it hurtled through space at an astonishing speed. Relative to the Sun, Comet 1 had a fairly average speed for a comet, a blinding forty kilometers per second. It would only take around two seconds for the comet to travel all the way from the upper stratosphere to sea level.

This made the actual event a bit anticlimactic since it would all happen so fast. Throughout the months when the comet fragments flew past Jupiter, Mars, and then the Moon, they became constant attractions in the night sky. Comet 1 had zoomed by the Moon only ten hours ago, the other two comets following close behind. Those two would continue past Earth . . . this time around.

Secretary Brighton, President Chaplin, and many others sat anxiously in the situation room, watching the projectors. Suri was there, too. She was recovering remarkably. She was now focused on the comet about to crash off the coast of France.

One of the U.S. government satellites' cameras was

trained on the probable impact site, and recorded the impact. It was difficult to see.

Those still in France would have seen a very bright light. Once the comet collided with the atmosphere, the friction with the surrounding air particles caused it to heat up tremendously. This caused the comet to get more luminous as it continued to travel through the atmosphere. The only thing the scientists back in New Mexico could see was a large white flash of light moving toward Earth. It entered the atmosphere at nearly ninety degrees—perpendicular to the Earth— and then, *boom.*

Almost immediately, the screen went dark.

"That's it?" President Chaplin asked. "What happened?"

Robert spoke up. "Most likely, the upper atmosphere has been severely ionized, disrupting our communications with the satellite. This could possibly last days. Additionally, it will take around thirty minutes for the seismic activity to reach us. The impact will trigger mass earthquakes and it is probable that these are the first effects we will feel."

They sat quietly, unsure of what to do. Some people made idle small talk. Then at thirty minutes, as if by clockwork, it felt as though the entire situation room was jolted violently up and there were loud crashing sounds all around. Immediately after that, Robert, in his wheeled chair, gripped the table as he swayed left and right. It felt as if the ground beneath them had turned to Jell-O. Then the lights went out.

• • •

Nestled far beneath the surface of the Earth, between columns of steel-reinforced concrete and amongst a large group of Americans, Karina and Dustin felt the first effects of the impact, what would later be reported as an 8.8 magnitude earthquake. The ground shook with such a violent ferocity that people screamed and cried out to God. People fell on top of each other and the bomb shelter quaked with a religious tenacity.

It even made Dustin pray, *Please God, please let's not get stuck down here.* Being claustrophobic did not help him.

Needless to say, everyone was very thankful when the shaking finally stopped. Someone asked the men at the door—Israeli soldiers holding their IWI Tavor TAR-21 assault rifles—if they would be allowed outside. Dustin listened to the soldier's straightforward answer with a mild chuckle.

"The ejecta, the rock and ground forced into the air by the impact, is going to superheat the Earth's atmosphere. A global firestorm, sir. If you go outside, you may be burned alive immediately. Unfortunately, no one will be allowed to leave for at least two months, as you may be cooked if you step outside."

"Oh," the man answered, turning a little red in the face before returning to sit with his family.

Dustin remembered his playing cards in his backpack. He got out the cards, and started to play gin with Karina. They would have a long time to go before they could go outside, but for now they were safe in Israel.

• • •

Jeremy and Anna sat together under Major Winter's mansion. Jeremy gave Anna a shoulder massage while they waited for some kind of effect from the impact. Jeremy looked around the dark tunnel where they sat. Major Winter nodded over at him when they made eye contact. There were more soldiers—maybe ten or so—and the rest looked like civilians. There was a large family of seven—two parents, a grandfather, and four kids. The kids were playing, and two cried and two laughed when they felt the ground move. The parents looked around nervously. An hour earlier, Major Winter had called a meeting and outlined the jobs that needed to get done in order to stay and live on the commune. Anna had volunteered to help with the indoor-farming operation, since she used to keep a garden with her mom before the comet.

Major Winter was a smart man. He had bought or otherwise acquired hundreds of gas-powered generators along with a massive amount of solar panels and batteries. He also had a large amount of UV lights, and had brought soil from the outside to fill up one of the underground rooms. He had all the material needed to build an indoor farm, complete with a wealth of seeds. He had tomatoes, onion, squash, zucchini, wheat, corn, and eggplant. He had actually gotten some tobacco as well, which Jeremy and Anna thought was a waste of space. Major Winter would not have it though, insisting they grow their own tobacco as well. "It's a cash crop; we may need it," he had said.

In addition to all the farming equipment, Major Winter had also stockpiled food staples to help them through the pre-harvest period, including flour, canned fruits and vegetables, salt, sugar, dried meats, and honey.

Jeremy was tasked with helping install the lighting and connecting it to the solar panels and the gas-powered generators. In fact, before the shaking had begun,

Jeremy had painstakingly covered all the solar panels with wood, so that they would not be damaged by the falling ejecta or a freak accident like a falling satellite. They also had extra solar panels stored underground that they could set up if the wood protection failed. Jeremy felt very thankful that he would be living out the "Nuclear Summer," as he liked to call it, at Major Winter's mansion instead of in the Lost River. He had not had high hopes for life there. He cried when he realized that so many people, and particularly Dustin and Karina, would perish within the next two months, but there was nothing he could do about it. He didn't even know if his parents had made it safely to the underground haven under Peters Mountain. All he could do was hope.

• • •

Janice paced through the artificial gravity wing of the Ark. The Ark had lost contact with Earth momentarily due to ionization of the stratosphere, and hadn't regained contact in the two days since the comet hit. Luckily, since the ship was above the normal orbiting range for satellites like the International Space Station—called Medium Earth Orbit—the ejecta from Comet 1's impact would not harm the Ark.

It took two weeks on the Ark for Janice to get entirely sick of the food. She realized that an extremely enjoyable part of her life had centered around food—cooking, tasting, and enjoying it. These were delicacies in her life, and they were unavailable for the foreseeable future.

Above all, she felt like she did not belong, but there wasn't anything she could do about that now. The lead scientist on the mission had told the members on the Ark that the two remaining comet fragments were still on a collision course with Earth, so they would need to stay on the Ark for at least five years to ensure their safety. The exact time depended of course on how well the teams of scientists on the ground did their jobs. Janice walked by the exercise room and the server room before stopping outside the computer room—a common workspace for many people on the Ark.

Janice saw a man she recognized, Alexander Chekhov, making some calculations. Janice and Alexander had been seated next to each other during the launch. She only knew him by name, and that they were close in age, and that he seemed to be shy. Alexander looked up when Janice peered into the room.

"It's astounding," he said to her in his lightly-accented English. "The impact has completely covered Earth with rock, dust, and minerals. It's completely black down there. I can't even see the continents, or clouds. It looks like a whole new planet . . . "

Janice walked away, unable to think of a response. She detested Alexander, though he had not done anything to deserve those feelings of animosity. Janice had thus far not made any friends on the Ark, and her father was not helping. He had noticed her crying in a side room a few hours before and had tried to comfort her.

"There, there, honey," he had cooed. "It had to be this way. We need to perpetuate the species. The world was too messed up, and life has a way of correcting organisms that can't live together. Humanity was already close to extinction before the comet, it was just a kind of self-inflicted extinction."

Janice's father rubbed her back before continuing, "I know how to cheer you up. You know that guy, Alexander? One of our computer programmers?"

"Yeah? What about him?"

"Well, he is actually very genetically diverse, and in the full body scan taken before launch, he is a very healthy individual."

"So?" Janice asked, confused.

"Sooo," her father replied, elongating the word, "you are also genetically diverse and healthy. It would be good for you two to get to know each other. You'll both have a lot of work to do once we touch back down on Earth."

"What are you talking about, Dad?"

"Procreation, sweetheart. You and Alexander are an

excellent match for each other, genetically speaking. You need to do your part for the human race, my daughter."

Disgusted, and trembling with rage, she got up and rushed off. Her father sighed, thinking that his daughter was going through a phase. Janice pushed through the series of doors and into the zero-gravity area of the Ark. There, she found a window, and floated next to it, looking out over the horizon of the Earth. Even though the entire world was obscured by a thick black veneer of rock and dust, it didn't make the view any less breathtaking. If only Janice could enjoy it.

4

HELP FROM AN UNLIKELY SOURCE

June 14, 2018, Vishnu Spacecraft, Medium Earth Orbit
Four Days Post-Impact

D*r. Nia Rhodes, Day 4 Post Impact*
It's been astounding watching the impact of Comet 1 from my spaceship. Since Comet 2 (the comet I'm orbiting) and Comet 3 have narrowly missed Earth, I had an excellent view of the impact using the telescope on my ship. I am closer to home than I've been since I left, but I've never felt farther away. It's lonely up here, and after losing contact with Earth after the impact, I thought it would be my last time communicating with anyone. But miraculously I've regained contact with New Mexico. This means I am able to speak with Gerald Jan as well as Dr. Miller and the rest of his team again.

It's nice speaking to Dr. Miller. He's really smart and surprisingly approachable. Gerald is smart too, but he's so . . . I don't know, particular? Yesterday he made sure I was roped in before I slept, otherwise I might drift off and hit something. The guy has never been in space before and I've been three times, and he's telling me to look out?

I cried yesterday when I realized how many of the people on Earth were going to die. There are a lot of people underground, and I heard that Russia has funneled fifty percent of its population underground. I guess their communist tendencies did end up paying off for the proletariat! The soot and ejected debris from the impact are returning to Earth now, as I can tell more light from the Sun is getting to Earth's surface.

I am so happy to have regained contact with Earth; it would be difficult to handle working alone all this time, especially for the upcoming six months. For the past six months I've been orbiting Comet 2, and our mission is moving along quite nicely. Unfortunately, since Comet 1's impact, NASA lost contact with the IMPs they sent to Comet 2. Luckily, I still have contact with them, so any adjustments that NASA or I find, I can send as instructions for the IMPs to change course.

It looks like the completion of the mission is in my hands. Or, in Vishnu's, anyways. I will use my data and Vishnu's nuclear devices to make sure Comet 2 does not impact Earth. I'm working through some modeling of Comet 2's orbital path as well, and I'm in contact with NASA again, but there are so many secondary effects which might occur on Earth that it's not certain I'll have contact the whole time.

On a slightly lighter note, I've decided to name the comets. Dr. Miller had named the original comet Shiva, after the Hindu god, but I will go with something else. The comet split into three, so I've decided to go with Greek mythology: Zeus, Poseidon, and Hades. Hades has already landed, and it has made Earth a living Hell. Zeus and Poseidon, or Comets 2 and 3 respectively, are looking to destroy it completely.

On the plus side, Zeus and Poseidon's new orbital paths continue to be very close to the Sun. This means that they are continuing to lose size due to the *sublimation of its ices, which I've noticed on Zeus—Comet 2—although it's not shrinking enough to save Earth. I have fifteen nuclear warheads on my ship, so combined with the twenty IMPs still on their way, we'd better hope they are enough.*

Regarding my television watching, I'm now on the show called The Big Bang Theory. *So far, I am not too excited about the physicists—it makes smart people seem so dumb! We aren't all social morons . . .*

• • •

Jeremy woke up in Major Winter's mansion to a tapping on his shoulder. He unwrapped his arms from around Anna, as they slept together on a small cot in one of the rooms built under Major Winter's mansion. It was stuffy in the room, and Jeremy rubbed his eyes, trying to make out what was happening. Someone was tapping him on the shoulder. When his eyes adjusted, he saw Major Winter standing over him.

"What's up, Major? Is there something wrong?"

"Come with me," Major Winter said.

Major Winter waited outside the room while Jeremy tugged on his sweatpants and a shirt. Anna's head popped out from under the covers, and she mumbled some indecipherable words—confusion at why she had been forced awake.

"Go back to sleep," Jeremy whispered, and kissed her on the forehead. She smiled and her head fell back onto her pillow.

Jeremy walked out of the room and looked at Major Winter, who held a flashlight in the dingy room, and was wearing a bulky backpack. Jeremy followed the hulking former Marine as they walked through the network of tunnels under the mansion. They stopped in front of a door with a large red sign that read, *DO NOT OPEN*. Jeremy could hear the hum of an engine coming from the other side of the door, but it sounded . . . different. He couldn't quite place it. Major Winter pulled a firefighter suit out of his backpack and put it on.

"Here," Major Winter said, giving Jeremy a suit of his own. "Put this on."

"What are we doing?" Jeremy asked, confused.

"You'll see."

Once they had suited up, Major Winter opened the airtight door and they stepped into an impossibly loud room. The floor of the room was covered with gas-powered generators, all lined up in neat little rows and chugging along. The room smelled of gasoline.

"Over here," the major yelled over the drone of the engines. "There's a vent and a shaft that eventually takes all the exhaust out to the atmosphere. You said you used to work for your father's contracting company, right?"

"Yeah!" Jeremy yelled. The roar of the engines had shaken him right awake.

"Well, over here," Major Winter walked to the north end of the room. "I've managed to wire some of the generators to our mainframe here. I was hoping you could help me finish?"

Jeremy nodded, taking a look at the entanglement

of wires in front of him. *Guess working for my father has come in handy after all*, Jeremy thought.

· · ·

Dustin and Karina were sequestered in an Israeli Defense Force nuclear bunker that had been excavated to allow enough room for three hundred people. The Israeli government had built enough of these for roughly half a million people to live. Dustin was truly astounded by what could be accomplished if the entire budget of a wealthy nation turned to solve a single problem. *If I wasn't so worried about the roof caving in . . .* Dustin thought.

Their particular bunker was simply one large room. The ceilings were uncomfortably low, and there were reinforced steel columns holding up the ground above them. There were mostly Israeli families in the bunker, which was called N17. So far, Dustin noticed that most of the families were keeping to themselves, and most of the survivors were praying often. There was a group of Hasidic Jews doing so in a corner. *We are so lucky to be alive*, Dustin thought.

It had been six days since the comet's impact and some news was filtering down to the bunker. The earthquakes had destroyed much of Israel's infra-structure as well as its cities and towns. The intense temperature increase had been over-exaggerated, though it was still far too hot to go outside. The impact had also caused Mount Ararat, the previously dormant volcano, to erupt, which only increased the amount of debris flung into the atmosphere. The ejected debris that was postulated to dramatically increase the temperature only blocked out the Sun for a week, and now it was clearing up, and light was returning to Earth. The volcanic eruption of Mount Ararat also caused a bout of acid rain in the area. Dustin and Karina were told all of this by a soldier on guard in their bunker.

"Did someone go up there to check?" Dustin had asked.

"We have scientists monitoring everything," the

soldier replied, "but they don't want to say exactly when civilians will be allowed above ground until they know more. For now, you can just wait."

Karina felt helpless and she hated to be told that there was nothing else she could do besides wait. She spent much of her time pacing back and forth and wondering what it was like for all those billions of people who didn't find refuge from the impact.

"Do you know," Karina asked the soldier, "what happened to the people above ground after the impact? Did they definitely die?"

"Anyone above ground would have had to find a place to go inside, otherwise they risk inhaling noxious fumes from the volcano, or the increase in temperature, or getting caught up in any of the fires that were ignited from the comet's impact. I'd say survival outside of underground bunkers is extremely unlikely."

Unlike Karina, Dustin tried not to think about the impact, preferring to live one day at a time. Dustin relished in the togetherness of their refugee status. He had even made friends with a guy named Ben. He was there with his family and was Israeli. He and Ben both shared a love for American football, which was surprising considering Ben grew up in Israel. He said his parents were farmers. Ben was ten years old, and wore simple clothing. He also wore a gold "chai" on a necklace outside of his T-shirt. Dustin learned that *chai* means *life* in Hebrew.

They sat against one of the large concrete columns drinking coffee and talking. Then, Ben spat his coffee out.

"I tried, Dustin, but I hate coffee. I don't get how you adults like it."

Ha! Dustin thought. *He thinks I'm an adult.*

"So, what do your parents do, Ben?" Dustin asked, smiling as Ben looked at his coffee cup in contempt.

"My parents are really good with plants," he began. "They don't use soil. They use water to feed the plants, and they make farming buildings for places like Japan that don't have a lot of room. Once we can go outside again, we are going to Norway!"

"What's in Norway?" Dustin asked.

"There's a place there that has every seed in the world, and they're all frozen! It's so amazing. My mom says they built this huge building. It sounds like an evil hiding place or the lair of a villain. Have you ever read *The Golden Compass*? They go to a place called Svalbard and that's where the seed place is. You should totally come with us! Svalbard sounds cool. Do you know they have polar bears there? I wonder if we'll see one."

Despite the playful way in which he spoke, Dustin was listening intently, thinking that it might be an excellent plan to go with Ben's family to Norway, if they let him. Ben's parents were surely going there to help develop some kind of post-comet farming technique or system. Maybe he and Karina could help? When Jeremy had decided to help after living in the Rockies, Dustin had felt a strong inclination to help as well, but had decided to go with Karina instead. Now, he felt differently. When Ben's parents called him back over to their side of the dungeon-like bunker, Dustin spoke with Karina.

"We should try to make friends with Ben's parents," he said in a hushed voice. "Did you hear that bit about the seeds in Svalbard? We could help them, and I'm sure they will need it. I'm sure that starvation is going to be a huge deal once we are allowed outside again. All the crops are probably burning right now, or died from acid rain or lack of sunlight."

"And," Karina added, "working with food means that you can feed yourself first. The best way to avoid starvation for us might be to go with them."

Dustin knew then that the two of them had found their next adventure. If only they could befriend this Israeli family they knew next to nothing about.

• • •

At the headquarters of the U.S. government in New Mexico, the seismic activity had died down, but it was still too hot for anyone to venture outside without the modified spacesuits. The ground team rejoiced when they found out that their communications were still live with Dr. Rhodes and the Vishnu spacecraft. Unfortunately, the LSST was non-operational after the impact catalyzed the eruption of a Chilean volcano named Cerro Azul. Robert and President Chaplin were playing cards together in the cafeteria, taking a brief mental-health break from making life and death decisions. They were playing poker, laughing, and betting against each other with unused shirt buttons.

Their laughter subsided when Secretary Brighton walked up, looking serious.

"Madam President, may I have a word in private?" he asked.

"Rob, I think Dr. Miller can hear whatever it is you have to say. I think we are a little beyond top-secret rules and regulations."

Secretary Brighton did not smile, but spoke quickly. "Kim Ha Lee from North Korea is on the phone."

"What? Are you serious? But their country is in anarchy," President Chaplin said, groaning. She did not want to hear from the unpredictable North Korean leader.

"I guess not, and the 'Supreme Leader' would like to speak to you. He says he thinks he may be able to help against the remaining comets."

President Chaplin looked over at Robert. She hadn't dyed her hair in months, and it was almost completely white, but despite her changing looks she still seemed very presidential.

"I guess that's the end of our mental-health break," she sighed.

"Go get 'em," Robert said, shuffling the cards and putting them back in their case. They were a deck of tourist playing cards, printed with picturesque photos of the Los Alamos hills.

President Chaplin and Secretary Brighton moved to the president's "office," a small room guarded by two Secret Service agents on either side of the door. The two politicians hovered over the phone. "Hello, Supreme Leader," President Chaplin said. "What can I do for you?"

"I want to offer my nation's services," Kim Ha Lee said in a French accent.

He was on speaker phone, and Chaplin looked over at Brighton, who looked back at her and then towards the phone again.

"I am listening, Supreme Leader. Your English has become much better."

Kim Ha Lee laughed. It was a nasal, hedonistic laugh. "Yes, I have been learning. Your country must be going through a lot right now, a lot of death."

"The comet has had a devastating impact on the entire world, it is true," the president answered diplomatically.

"Yes, yes. I am calling because for the past three years, we have been developing missiles to launch against the comet J312. They will be ready by the next launch phase in three months."

President Chaplin and Secretary Brighton looked at each other, surprised.

"Supreme Leader, that is great news indeed. Deflecting the comets will be very difficult. We would appreciate any help we can get. Thank you for this offer."

"You are very welcome, Mrs. President."

Madam President, President Chaplin thought, but decided not to correct the enigmatic dictator.

"My chief engineer, Kang Sok Ju, will reach out to your team soon. And, Mrs. President?"

Aha, President Chaplin thought. *Now we're getting to it.* What would the Supreme Leader of North Korea require for his cooperation? "Yes, Supreme Leader?" she asked, practically holding her breath.

"I would like the Democratic People's Republic of Korea to be a permanent part of the U.N. Security Council."

Chaplin and Brighton looked at each other, reading each other's thoughts. Brighton even had to keep himself from laughing. The governing body of the United Nations had been nonexistent for the last two years. The U.N. had tried to involve itself in the projects against the comet, but its complex bureaucracy had forced it to move at a snail's pace, and thus countries like the United States and Russia quickly left it behind. Also, with anarchy running wild in much of the world, international conflicts were nearly non-existent, so nations turned inward to try and stave off the chaos.

Having North Korea as a permanent member of the U.N. Security Council would certainly have caused conflict before the comet. After, if the world did manage to survive another year, who knew what would happen? Perhaps a new United Nations would be created. In any event, President Chaplin—and probably everyone else in the world—thought the fate of the world was ultimately worth having North Korea be put on the Security Council. As president, Victoria Chaplin was used to making empty promises.

"Of course, Supreme Leader. I should be able to make this happen. Let's get Dr. Miller in contact with Mr. Kang and we will go from there. Thank you very much."

"Thank you, Mrs. President."

Chaplin hung up the phone, and looked crossly at Brighton.

"Do you think we can trust North Korea?" the president asked.

"Definitely not," Brighton responded, "and who's to say they'll even have facilities up to the standards of successfully shooting IMPs into space?"

"Too good to be true, maybe," Chaplin admitted.

"At the same time," Brighton mused, "we could use any help we can get. I'm sure it will be advantageous for Robert. He'll be able to use their missiles. In fact, we should send a team there to inspect their launch facility, just to see. But we have to be careful of Kim Ha Lee, they may try something."

When Secretary Brighton told Robert the news, he immediately began to plan a trip to Korea. It gave him something new to focus on. He made an appointment to speak on the phone with the engineer from North Korea, and went to tell Suri about the new plan.

Suri was also feeling much better. She completed a rigorous therapy program for her legs daily. They had atrophied from her time of inactivity, but she was beginning to walk again. Her brain was as sharp as before her accident, though there were still bits and pieces of her memory which were gone, like missing puzzle pieces. She could see all around the foggy recollections, but when it came to the memories themselves, some still drifted out of reach.

Suri learned that a terrorist had bombed the airplane, and that the terrorist adhered to the premise that humans should not intervene in the work of God and that Judgment Day had come. She learned that the plane had started taxiing down the runway when it exploded, and that she was the sole survivor. She even learned that being seated in the very back of the plane had saved her. When it came to her own memories of that moment, however, everything was dull and fuzzy. She didn't even remember waking up the morning of the bombing.

Suri tried her best to not think about her lost memories and focus on work.

Robert told her about North Korea. However, they

hadn't spoken to their scientists yet, so there was no way of knowing how much help they would actually be. They had six months before the other two comets were slated to come into contact with Earth again, but Comet 2 would be their sole focus. At twenty kilometers in diameter, this one had the potential to finish the annihilation that the first impact started.

Their communications with Dr. Nia Rhodes aboard Vishnu were luckily back online. However, the increased temperatures on Earth could eventually cause some of the communication units to fry. They also had a few IMPs and standalone nuclear bombs left, and now they had North Korea—though what value this added remained uncertain.

Gerald Jan and many of his top engineers had flown in from Los Angeles to work alongside NASA as well, and they were offering a great deal of assistance in the effort.

The Los Alamos team was working to have a plan ready within three months that would hopefully defeat Comet 2. Since the orbits of Comets 2 and 3 were so elongated, they were closer to the Sun than in their entire orbital year. This meant the Sun would melt their frozen exteriors, shrinking their size and resulting in a much smaller impact. Unfortunately, the nuclei of both comets were still made up of rock, making them potentially deadly no matter how much ice melted.

Dr. Rhodes had called the comets Zeus and Poseidon, which Suri found easier to handle than Shiva. Zeus was much larger, and Poseidon small enough to basically ignore, even though its impact would still cause significant damage. The team in Los Alamos had not yet received any information on the status of the Atlantic seaboard, but by now the tsunami caused by Comet 1's impact had, in all likelihood, destroyed Cape Canaveral, making it unusable as a launch site. The tsunami would also stop boats from delivering raw materials from Africa and Europe, making building more IMPs much more difficult. They would have to make do with what they had.

The remaining IMPs, held previously at Houston or Cape Canaveral, had been moved to the Denver

International Airport, which was the one part of Colorado still under U.S. government control. With the rising temperatures, there would probably be no problem with anarchist or terrorist groups trying to stop them from saving the world. They were all hiding out somewhere worrying about their survival.

At least I hope so, Suri thought. *We better not have to fight another war against ourselves while we try to save the world.*

5

MUCH ADO ABOUT SOMETHING

June 18, 2018, Major Winter's Mansion, Texas
Eight Days Post-Impact

Jeremy took off the firefighter suit required for his new job as engine room electrician. He was almost done wiring their living quarters and had also wired a grow room. Everyone living in Major Winter's little commune had to work—and Anna was working on germinating seeds in damp paper towels. She sat in a room with another woman, a large and friendly southerner named Tabatha. She was originally from Mississippi and before the comet hit, had been a nurse. Anna and Tabatha's job was to place four seeds in between two of the damp paper towels, put them in plastic bags, zip them up, and then stick them into a temperature-controlled box set at seventy-five degrees Fahrenheit.

Jeremy watched Anna label a box "tomatoes." She had completed two boxes already: "Super Sweet 100" and "Napa Grape."

"Oh, good morning. Where were you working today?" she asked, jotting down her actions in a notebook.

"Engine room wiring," Jeremy answered, bending down to kiss Anna.

"Everything set up? I'll need to start giving these guys some light in a few days," Anna remarked, finishing a box containing Anna's favorite tomato, the Golden Nugget.

"I'll have it ready by then."

"Good," Anna said. "In a few months, we'll be up to our ears in tomatoes!"

• • •

Janice was doing yoga in the exercise room on the

Ark when Alexander, her prospective mate according to her father, walked awkwardly into the room. She pretended not to notice him and continued to not notice him put his own yoga mat a few paces away from hers. The exercise room of the Ark was one of the larger rooms with artificial gravity in the spaceship. These rooms were important. When people spent a lot of time in zero gravity, it affected their body in many ways. Human bodies evolved for Planet Earth, and being in zero gravity had adverse effects on the body. For example, a lot of muscles—like back muscles and calf muscles—were mainly used to fight the effect of gravity. In space, those muscles could atrophy. And all the spaceship inhabitants wanted to be able to walk again once they could repopulate the Earth.

For this reason, everyone on board the Ark was supposed to be working out like they were trying to look like Arnold Schwarzenegger during his body-building days. Aside from working out, Janice also practiced yoga to keep her body limber. It also helped relax her mind. Janice was in a Sarvangasana pose, also known as Standing Shoulder. The back of her neck was parallel to the floor and she had pushed up her lower torso and legs straight in the air. Her elbows and triceps, combined with her neck, made the base. It was not a simple position. It had taken Janice weeks to perfect it, and she paused in it now, able to focus on her breathing in the pose.

As she counted her breaths, she watched in mild humor as Alexander tried to copy her pose. He shook dramatically and wobbled back and forth a few times before falling over. The fourth time he tried he got his legs elevated, but then his momentum caused him to roll backwards painfully over his neck.

"Hmph," he said as his body collided with the floor, opposite his yoga mat.

Janice felt sorry for the guy.

"Maybe try something easier first?" Janice asked, turning her head calmly to the lump of Russian beside her.

"Yes, I think so, too," Alexander replied.

He switched into a tree pose, standing on one leg

with the heel of his other pressing into his thigh as high as possible.

He stood there for another minute—trying his best to remain upright—before speaking. "My father is an oligarch. He is friends with Vladimir Putin, and the only reason I am here is because of him. I am a good computer programmer, but nowhere near the best in the world. I did not ask to be born to my father, and I did not ask to be put on this ship. I am sorry we are here together . . . I think my father told me the same thing that yours told you."

Surprised, Janice looked over at Alexander and then back to the wall in front of her.

"I think you are right," she said evenly.

Janice switched into a Chakra Sana pose, or the Upward Facing Bow or Wheel pose, and Alexander tried several times to begin a sentence, before starting over and then saying, "Well, I just wanted to say I know this is probably not easy, and I will not make things more difficult for you. I'm guessing both of us do not want to be here."

With that, Alexander nodded and smiled at Janice, picked up his yoga mat, and departed the artificial gravity room. Janice watched him go, thinking she might have just made a friend.

• • •

Vishnu Spacecraft . . .

Dr. Nia Rhodes, Eight Days Post-Impact: I have just finished the episode of How I Met Your Mother *titled "The Pineapple Incident" and it reminded me of college. People think that engineers are all nerds and we stay in on Friday nights and play World of Warcraft, but that's not true. Of course, a lot of my classmates did just that, but I remember many Saturday and Sunday mornings where I had to recount the night with my friends to remember what we did. Work hard, play hard. Don't get me wrong, I studied really hard in college, and working for SpaceX has been the hardest—and most fun—job of my entire life.*

I didn't have what you would call a 'normal' life, but

I guess no astronaut does. But it's not like I can change it now. I was in love once, though. Ugh. Why am I writing this? The psychologist told me to write all my thoughts down if I was feeling anxious, but reading it now makes me seem like an angst-filled teenager again. Hold on—I need to run a quick diagnostic check on the oxygenator.

Okay, I'm back. No more ranting about love. Thus far the Earth has been clearing up nicely. It was almost black within a day after impact, but it's been getting steadily lighter since, and now I think visibility has returned to around fifty percent of pre-impact levels. I can see some bright red light coming around latitude fifty-one. I assume this is the crater, and the red is molten rock from the impact. I've been sending all of my data to New Mexico as well, of course. They postulated it would take around two to three weeks for all that ejecta and debris to return to Earth. That will cause the most harm. Some scientists thought that the debris might be light enough to remain in the atmosphere, which would block out the Sun for years or decades. That would destroy almost all life on Earth, though seeds could lie dormant for a time, and *there are certain prokaryotes that live without sunlight that would survive.*

California, the eastern seaboard, and much of Western Europe were completely devastated by the tsunamis that hit both coasts. I'm keeping an eye on the polar ice caps as well, which are melting at a predictable rate, though probably it will take a few years for them to melt completely. Being this "fly on the wall" is so fascinating, yet so depressing. It's sad to watch our beautiful Earth suffer . . .

6

NEW FRIENDS

June 20, 2018, San Antonio Mountain
Ten Days Post-Impact

Much of the debris that was ejected into the atmosphere went all the way into Low Earth Orbit, compromising all space-based communication. This unfortunate circumstance forced Robert and Suri to speak with Dr. Kang Sok Ju, Chief Engineer of North Korea's National Aerospace Development Administration, over the phone, through the trans-Pacific cable that connects the Korean peninsula with the United States. Since Dr. Kang did not speak English, a deep-voiced translator was on the line with them. He introduced himself as Mr. Yuan.

"Dr. Kang, my name is Dr. Robert Miller. I'm the Chief Scientist for NASA. How are you?"

"It's nice to meet you, Dr. Miller."

Robert thought he could detect a Swiss, or perhaps German accent. *He must have gone abroad to boarding school or university*, Robert thought.

The translator continued, "I will begin by telling you we plan to be independent from NASA in defeating the comets. We have been working on this project for quite some time. We would like to coordinate with your efforts so our missiles do not intersect, and we are willing to offer you a facility where you may launch your missiles as well."

Suri and Robert exchanged uneasy glances at each other. *I thought they wanted to work with us?* Robert thought.

Robert answered, "You've been working without the help of any other countries?"

"That's correct. The Supreme Leader, in his infinite wisdom, did not want us to use our nuclear warheads unless it was absolutely necessary for the survival of the planet."

"Dr. Kang, our Air Force bases in both California and Florida are unusable at the moment, and manufacturing Interplanetary Missiles in new facilities has not yet been accomplished. We would like to cooperate with you, and can bring you additional nuclear warheads to use at your airfield."

The translator spoke rapidly to Dr. Kang, who then spoke with a third individual, and all three voices spoke to each other in unnecessarily hushed tones. Secretary Brighton, also in the room, pushed the mute button on the phone, and spoke to Robert and his team.

"Robert, you don't have authorization to give nuclear missiles to North Korea! That is something we are going to have to discuss."

Robert looked angrily at the Secretary of State. "Nick. This is not a political issue. This is a life-or-death issue. This is not something we can ignore. We need a launch facility. Without more impact to Comet

2, there won't be a world to defend against North Korea."

Robert unmuted the conversation and the translator's voice came in the room.

"Dr. Miller? Are you there?"

"Yes, sorry. Could you repeat, please?"

"What do you mean by cooperate?" the translator asked.

"Well, I would like to be involved in the deployment process and decision making. I believe that Dr. Kang and I should have the final say together," Robert said, trying to be convincing, before adding, "Two minds are better than one, right, Doctor?"

Again there was a flurry of Korean. Robert imagined them saying something along the lines of "depends on which minds," and Robert looked over at President Chaplin, who had entered the room at the beginning of the conversation, remaining in the background. She nodded in agreement with Robert, thinking it would be smart, but quickly wrote something down on a piece of paper and showed it to

Robert. On it was written, *Say you want to go to North Korea.*

Finally, the translator spoke again in English, "Dr. Miller. We will agree to your terms. Do you have access to a ship?"

"I will discuss with the president and we will find something that will work for all of us."

"Very well, Dr. Miller."

Once they got off the phone, Secretary Brighton turned to President Chaplin.

"Victoria," he began, surprising Robert by using her first name. "You can't think that sending nuclear weapons to North Korea could be a good idea."

"No, Nick. I agree—it's a bad idea," President Chaplin sighed. "Unfortunately, it's the best bad idea we have. Robert, when the temperature returns to a level where Air Force One can safely deliver you to Pyongyang, you'll go. We'll send a team of Marines with you to protect you. Meanwhile, I want you to work on a strategy against Comet 2 that involves being able to send more IMPs to divert its course. Speak with Dr. Rhodes as well, and apprise her of the news."

• • •

Dr. Raymond Kaser sat in his office in the Ark. He was meditating, concentrating on his breathing and the expansion of his lungs. He was sitting down on a chair, which was a luxury on the large spaceship orbiting Earth. As the man who started the Ark project, he had the only office in the artificial gravity wing of the ship. After fifteen minutes of breathing exercises, Raymond opened his eyes. It was seventeen hundred hours on their thirteenth day orbiting Earth. Raymond started to look over some diagnostics to ensure all was running smoothly. In front of him he also had the chemical compositions of the remaining two comets. Both of them had enormous amounts of rhodium, platinum, and rhenium. Dr. Rothschild, one of Raymond's chief engineers, sat across the desk from him, nervously twiddling his thumbs.

"So, if there's any way to kick the comets into a stable orbit, we should try. It would be worth it to have these massive reserves of raw material less than a quarter of a million miles away."

"Thank you, Dr. Rothschild," Raymond said, "I will take this into consideration. Please bring in Mr. Chekhov's son, Alexander."

"Thank you, sir. I will, sir."

With a bow, the doctor left the office. Shortly after, there was a knock at the door.

"Come in."

An anxious-looking Russian walked in with messy hair and an almost indecipherable accent.

"Hello, Mr. Kaser," Alexander said.

"You have the logs for me?" Raymond asked, switching his attention to moving files around his desk.

"I sent it, yes."

Raymond picked up his tablet from the table and opened the file that Alexander had just emailed him. It was a communications log between the Ark and Earth. Alexander tapped his foot on the ground while Raymond looked over the documents. Finally, Alexander broke the silence.

"I'm sure you noticed the lack of communication between two hours after impact and now."

"Of course, Mr. Chekhov. Why do you think I called you in here? I need information about how and why this happened."

"Yes, well. I think that there was an intense amount of ionized particles that were ejected, meaning there was a lot more noise on our communications than before. Basically, no one had any communication for twenty-three hours. Once those regions of the atmosphere deionized, our communications came back online. I monitored what happened during those twenty-three hours, and it appears that our bases around the world are stable. Unfortunately, we do not have communications with North America, though South America, Africa, and Europe are all online. Israel is still out of communication as well . . . " Alexander shifted uncomfortably in his seat.

"And our bunkers are all operational? Those out of the blast radius are still usable?"

"Yes, sir. Those bunker locations on the eastern seaboard, as well as the Caribbean and eastern South America have likely been hit with tsunamis, but the engineers accounted for this possibility in their design, and they are equipped with ventilation systems."

"Very well, Mr. Chekhov, thank you for your time. You may go."

Raymond did not watch Alexander get up and walk out of the room, for he was already considering Dr. Rothschild's idea of bringing the comets into orbit.

It could be the start to the New World that we need. It would be good to have these mineral and metal reserves while we repopulate and rebuild the Earth, Raymond thought. He was intrigued by the comets' potential raw materials load—particularly the smallest comet fragment—though how he could harvest it after blasting it to bits with nuclear weapons he didn't know. Raymond was the only person who could launch their two warheads, as the launch button required a password, which only he knew, plus his own finger-print and an iris scan.

Raymond Kaser had come up with the plan for the Ark when one of his Russian business partners had told him about the massive comet hurtling towards them. They were in his private jet traveling from Moscow to his home in Manhattan.

"How large is it?" Raymond had asked.

"If nothing is done, it will destroy all life on Earth."

Raymond had not slept for two days after the Russian told him this. He was entrenched in thought about what to do, but eventually decided that it may be a blessing in disguise. He had always believed that only the über-rich had the power to change the world. Raymond decided that if the comet were to hit, he would be certain to not be on Earth. Then he thought about the state of the Earth, and how global warming, rampant corruption, and greed were destroying the planet. In fact, a lot of this had actually helped him rise to power.

And so, his plan to build the Ark was born. Over

the course of its construction, Raymond had decided that there was a silver lining to the Earth being rid of most of its human population. It could be a clean slate for Earth—a way to start over.

Making difficult choices was what Raymond did for a living, and he could see the direction in which the world was turning. The problems of the world could not be fixed simply by creating some recycling programs, or affirmative action. Large scale, global, radical change needed to occur, and luckily this comet came at just the right time.

Raymond always had friends in high places, as his father did before him. Raymond came from a long line of industrialists dating back to the fifteenth-century French aristocracy. When he had reached out to build the Ark, many of his closest business partners had asked to help in the effort, in exchange for a spot on the ship. These were people who shared his want for creating a new world. Part of his plan was to build underground lairs so some chosen people who remained on Earth could outlast the impact event.

He also had built bunkers loaded with supplies and repopulating kits—seeds and water filtration equipment, tools, medical supplies, books.

I can rebuild the world with a new grand image, Raymond thought. *No poverty, no overpopulation, no environmental destruction.* While overlooking the blackened atmosphere of Earth through his office window, Raymond thought about all the potential greatness his New World Order could provide.

• • •

Karina ate her lunch alone in their underground hideout in Tel Aviv. Dustin was busy trying to network with Ben and his parents. Karina looked around at their bunker while eating some rice and beans, the Israeli post-apocalyptic staple. It had now been ten days since the impact. They were told that it would take seven more weeks for the temperature of the Earth to cool to a reasonable level. It was currently over seven hundred degrees Celsius, and over the course of seven weeks the heat would gradually return to normal, pre-comet levels, and based on some scientist's prediction it was possible it would dip below, since the volcanic explosions catalyzed by the comet's impact released a lot of chemicals which would cool the Earth's temperature.

Despite the good news about the temperature, the devastated Earth would indeed look incredibly bleak. Europe would be totally destroyed, and the rest of the world would not fare well either. The falling debris and extreme temperatures would destroy much of the vegetation on Earth. The earthquakes that occurred shortly after the impact had apparently already decimated much of the world's infrastructure, and the massive volcanic activity could even create new islands in the Pacific Rim. Extreme weather patterns were likely to affect the entire globe for years after the initial impact.

Karina thought about this as she ate her meal. She noticed that, as she was in the corner of the cafeteria, there was only one person eating at her table. She was an older woman, and the only one in the complex wearing a headscarf. She picked at her food solemnly. As Dustin was busy making friends, Karina tried to give it a shot.

"Hey, what's your name?" she asked the woman.

"Fatima," the woman said curtly.

"I'm Karina," she offered, trying to break the woman's walls a bit to make a new friend. "It's pretty lucky that we got here, isn't it?"

Fatima was dressed in a light-brown headscarf and a black shirt. She looked up at Karina then back down at her food.

"Where are you from, Karina?"

"America."

"Figures. What nationality do you think I am?"

"Um, Israeli?"

"Palestine. I'm from Palestine. The only reason I am here is because my husband and I live in Israel and our son fights in the Israeli Defense Force, despite our attempts to get him not to. I had to watch while my people were systematically kicked out of a place we'd called home for thousands of years.

"I've had friends of mine explain to authorities that they would be killed if they went back to their home countries of Syria, Afghanistan, Iraq. The governments of the West just looked the other way as people were killed, or actually participated in the killing. I've had friends who actually translated and worked for Western governments, the United States and Great Britain, and when they needed to get out of the country because people wanted to kill them . . . those very same governments denied their applications.

"Now I watch all you people, yes, I mean you people, just go underground in a foreign country, traveling across borders that are permanently closed to people that look like me. The only reason I'm here is because I am in love with a Jewish Israeli who happens to fight on our side. But I look around this room and I see more Europeans and Americans than Arabs or even Israelis. Your privilege and your passports have gotten you to live another day in this world of ours, and that is nothing new. Please do not try to make friends with me, little girl. You should not be here. But when things get bad all your 'rules,' all your 'borders,' they just all go by the wayside, don't they?"

Karina blinked, unsure what to say. She could *feel* the venom in this woman's voice.

"But I don't expect you to understand." Fatima spoke this last sentence with disgust and contempt. She stood up and walked away from her tray of food, briskly disappearing through the cafeteria.

That didn't go as planned, Karina thought, sighing.

• • •

Anna thought the garden looked gorgeous. She would even go so far as to call it *her* garden, since she had become a main decision maker in the process. It felt good to be doing something helpful, just like when she worked in the manufacturing plant making the computer chips for the IMPs. Her underground garden had three large forty-watt heat lamps over each bed of soil. Nothing had truly started to grow yet, but Tabatha and Craig followed her actions as they continued making beds for as many UV lamps as they had.

"My mother was a biologist," she explained when Craig had asked where she learned gardening, "and when I was young she would take me to work with her sometimes. She researched microbiology and fungi. We would always have a garden of our own in the spring."

Suddenly, when she looked down at the soil bed in front of her, she became incredibly nauseous, and immediately vomited on the topsoil.

"Oh, honey!" Tabatha said, rubbing her back. "Are you alright? Did you eat an expired MRE or something?"

"I haven't eaten in a few hours," Anna said, confused. *MRE's don't expire for years either* . . . Anna thought.

She wiped her mouth, confused, and excused herself to go to the bathroom to clean up and brush her teeth.

7

CHECKPOINT

July 6, 2018, Medium Earth Orbit, Ark Spacecraft
Twenty-Six Days Post-Impact

Janice sat in the computer room, strapped to the chair in front of a computer. Since Janice was adept at computer programming, there was a lot of work she could do on the Ark. Currently, she sat inputting personal data for its passengers. Basically, once the five years on the Ark were up, the group would go back down to Earth, and depending on where they landed, they would make their way to one of a hundred-or-so "checkpoints" which were strategically placed around the world. These checkpoint locations were bunkers, filled with things like food, gasoline, and essential materials that the Ark survivors would need. Each checkpoint also kept a large military grade Humvee, and some weapons. There were some larger checkpoints, which also had helicopters and multiple rooms, suitable to work to create this true New World Order.

Because their landing location on Earth was unknown, Raymond Kaser had built these checkpoints all over the Earth. He also wanted to make sure that if by some miracle the scientists managed to divert the course of the comet, non-Ark survivors would not be able to use the checkpoints' resources. To accomplish this, he made sure that only the passengers on the Ark could get into the checkpoint bunkers. Since they were already fingerprinted and biometrically identified as part of their agreement to come onto the Ark, they could use their fingerprints or a password to get into each of the one hundred checkpoints around the world. The only thing that remained was inputting the biometric information of the passengers into the password slots for the checkpoint bunkers. This was where Janice came in, whose job it was to input this data. Knowing the passwords to enter the checkpoints might be the way she could atone for the damage she had done by helping the terrorist bomb the plane. She wasn't sure how it would work yet, but perhaps a plan would form soon.

She worked while listening to her favorite music, the Arctic Monkeys, with headphones. After an hour or so, Alex Chekhov came swimming into the room and strapped himself in. He brought a small water pouch, and headphones of his own, putting them in his ears. The water pouch had a Velcro back, and he stuck it next to the keyboard, which was also Velcroed to the ground. Janet had quickly learned that Velcro was everywhere in space. Janice noticed Alex only inserted one headphone, allowing her the opportunity to speak if she wanted. To reciprocate this small gesture, she did the same. After a few minutes of work, Janice spoke up.

"So, what does the Man have you doing?"

Alex smiled, entering a few lines of code before turning to look at her.

"It's pretty cool, actually. When this ship goes back

to Earth, the communications satellite and some of the components of the artificial gravity room will stay in orbit. They will function as a sort of new satellite, and they will push themselves farther away from Earth, into a geosynchronous orbit.

"It will tell us where to land, and where all the checkpoint locations are relative to us. Each passenger will have a small GPS with positioning points, and it will tell them where to go for the checkpoints. I have been working on this software for a while now; it wasn't ready before we launched. I have to write the code for the positioning points."

"Oh, that's cool. Have you done something like that before?" Janice asked politely.

"I worked for the Russian communications ministry, so I have some experience. It is difficult, though, because I can only artificially test my design, since the satellite isn't working yet."

Janice thought for a moment.

"Can I see?"

"The code? Sure."

Janice looked over Alex's code. It looked complicated and impressive. It was in a language she was unfamiliar with, but she could identify some of its aspects. Suddenly she had an idea.

"Where are the checkpoint locations?"

"All around the world; there are around a hundred of them, I think."

"Can I see where they are?"

Alex considered for only one second before saying yes. The chairs in the computer room were on rails below them, so they could shift laterally alongside the row of computers. Janice slid herself over toward Alex so she could see his screen. Janice looked over the map, seeing checkpoints all around the world pinned on a map with a gold pin. Since the checkpoints were built before anyone knew where the comet would hit, there were some in Europe, which would probably look more like molten lava than survival resources, but they were pinned all the same. There were checkpoints in Israel, Brazil, Mexico, South Africa, Australia—there was even one on Antarctica.

"Most of them are inland, since Mr. Kaser decided that it would be wise in case the comet landed in water and caused a tsunami. It was actually the most likely place for it to land, since around seventy percent of Earth is covered in water. It's a terrible wonder that the small part of it hit so close to one of the most populous areas in the world . . . "

As Alex's voice drifted off, Janice asked for a screenshot of the image. Alex agreed and sent it to her.

A woman is always able to manipulate a lonely man in her midst, Janice thought. *I have checkpoint locations, and the passwords to get into them. How can I use this?*

• • •

Dr. Nia Rhodes, One month post-Impact:

Well, hello again. Everything here on Vishnu is going well, and I've used four of my nuclear bombs to move the comet—but so far it has not shifted enough. Five months before Comet 2, codename Zeus, will wreak havoc on Earth.

My muscles are beginning to atrophy severely, but I do have my very own artificial gravity room. Here I spend most of my time trying to keep the amount of muscle tone I have left. The Earth is looking much healthier with each day that passes. Much of the dust has settled (excuse the literal idiom!). I just traveled over the impact zone, which is still bright red. England and France have been completely destroyed. The same goes for much of western Europe. Even from space I can see the devastation of the massive earthquakes, volcanic activity, the primary effects of the impact, and the resulting tsunamis. The Gulf of Mexico was partially protected by Florida, but South America was hit hard. The impact crater looks to be around twenty-five miles wide. The lush green color of western Europe as seen by space is sadly no more; a solemn gray has taken over. There was a large tsunami that originated east of New Zealand, which must have resulted from the comet penetrating the Earth's crust. This large megatsunami hit the western coast of both North and South America. The Andes Mountains in South America acted as an effective barrier, shielding inland

Brazil, but Chile's coastal cities were devastated. Also, two of their volcanoes erupted due to the comet's impact. Central America and Mexico, as well as the western United States were also hit hard by the tsunami.

One interesting note that I did not expect is the increase in islands in the Pacific Ocean due to the increase in volcanic activity from the comet's impact. Many of those islands in Earth's biggest ocean are simply underwater volcanoes, and near French Polynesia I have spotted a new island beginning to form. I have taken the liberty of naming this island "Nia Island." I would have used my last name but that one has already been taken—it's an island in Greece.

Oh, and I almost forgot! In addition to the four nuclear missiles sent from Vishnu, I successfully directed six IMPs to hit Comet 2, Zeus. Unfortunately, it's still on target to hit Earth. More work needs to be done.

• • •

After three weeks, the temperatures around Los

Alamos had decreased to around one hundred and forty-five degrees Fahrenheit—by no means cold, but just cool enough to allow Robert to travel. He'd need protective clothing, but the journey over the Pacific to North Korea was given the green light. President Chaplin called together a meeting of the heads of each of the anti-impact teams in New Mexico to discuss preparations. Chaplin stood at the head of the largest table in the cafeteria. It was the only room big enough to house what remained of NASA and the efforts to stop the comets.

"We have a little more than two months before we must resume an effective launch schedule. Since we relocated back to New Mexico from St. Thomas, we have been working on building a space launch station here. We tried to build one as quickly as possible, but sadly there is too much to do and it is my belief that our best decision is to move all of our IMPs to an alternate station. That station is in North Korea. Kim Ha Lee has a functioning launch station that we will use to launch our remaining IMPs toward the comets."

President Chaplin let that sink in as not everyone had known that this was the plan. Robert, Suri, and Secretary Brighton looked around to see who would be most surprised by this unlikely alliance. General Diaz was beside himself with anger.

"We can't trust North Korea! Are you crazy? They will try to take over the world."

"Unfortunately, we don't have a choice. There won't be a world to take over if we don't have a place to launch our defense systems." Chaplin had decided not to mention to General Diaz that she had promised Kim Ha Lee a permanent seat on the U.N. Security Council if the world survived the comets.

Suri watched in awe as the members of Congress lucky enough to be brought to New Mexico almost unilaterally opposed the idea. It felt to her like these people still thought there was such an entity as the "United States of America." It was as if everyone had forgotten that the world was so close to destruction—and that so much of it had been destroyed already. Suri had decided a long time ago not to stick her head in the way of the politicians, and instead simply let them make their choices. She would work on the science, and hopefully, with a bit of luck, they could avoid total catastrophe again. She tuned back in when she heard her own name.

"Dr. Robert Miller will go with the IMPs and our supplies, along with some military personnel, on a ship to North Korea, where Kim Ha Lee has built a launch site protected from the effects of the comet. Suri Lahdka will run operations from here alongside Dr. Samuel Olidi and Mr. Jan. I am happy to have Mr. Jan's expertise on hand, and I hope you all join me in welcoming him to formally begin working for the United States of America."

A brief round of applause ensued as Gerald Jan stood up and smiled. Suri thought he looked a lot paler and a little sickly, but chalked it up to the stress that the comet had placed on everyone. Gerald Jan had been working alongside NASA as a helpful go-between with the Vishnu spacecraft, as he and his team knew the most about its capabilities. However, Gerald would now be present and informed of all of NASA's operations from Los Alamos, as Robert and his hand-selected team would go to North Korea.

Suri just hoped that with his help, they could defeat the remaining comets.

• • •

Jeremy sat across from Major Winter in the largest of the underground rooms, the cafeteria. They had finished lunch and were playing chess. Jeremy sat staring at the chessboard, one hand on his temple as he tried to think of his next move. He was playing the white pieces, which meant that he'd made the first move. This meant that he had an advantage, but doubted that would help him defeat his enemy. Major Winter was an excellent chess player. In the week and a half that they played against each other, Jeremy had not won a single game.

Life underground was mundane. He worked as much as he could, but there were only so many times he could organize the food or repair electric appliances. The wiring project was completed, but aside from being in charge of refilling the generators in the engine room every eight hours or so, he had more time on his hands than ever. He tried not to think about the people who had perished in the heat—the people who had not found places to go underground, and not having anything to do definitely made this more difficult. Jeremy prayed that his parents had made it to the Denver bunker, and that—against all odds—Dustin and Karina had found their own safe haven somewhere far away from the impact site.

"So, what are you going to do when the temperature returns to a reasonable level?" Major Winter asked. "It should happen pretty soon—a month maybe? Personally I welcome all those here to stay if they choose, but we will begin trying to rebuild infrastructure. I know you might feel bored now, but try to enjoy it. Boredom means security, and that can be a lot nicer than action depending on what type of excitement you have."

"I'm really not sure," Jeremy replied, looking up from the board. "I hope that I'll be able to help in the fight against the other two comets."

"Yes, I forgot for a second they're still coming," Major Winter said, much to Jeremy's surprise. "What do you think will happen?"

"It will be hard because I bet a lot of the missile-launching material is broken or completely destroyed. I know that we have some of the IMPs stored underground, but we definitely don't have the means to make any more before the comets come close to us again. We also have the spaceship Vishnu orbiting the Earth, and it has a lot of IMPs on it, and that should help, too. I think it's probably our best hope."

"Yes, that's probably true," the major replied, moving a rook forward and putting Jeremy into check.

"I don't know, Major. I try not to think about it, but it seems like we are running out of options."

8

A RELATIVE COLD FRONT

August 8, 2018 San Antonio Mountain
Approximately Seven Weeks Post-Impact

Suri looked at herself in the mirror. She was even skinnier than before the bombing, and her face felt thin and stretched. Her arms and legs felt weak, but the physical therapy helped. *If only there was some real food here*, she thought. *I'd be able to regain some of the muscle I'd lost.* Her face had deep scars on it, as did her arms. The only scar that bothered her was thick and long, trailing from her right ear down to her shoulder and then curling down her back. She put on a scarf to hide it, grimaced, and walked down to the cafeteria.

She felt honored to work with Dr. Olidi, a brilliant Nigerian who had gone to Harvard and had a

PhD in astrobiology. He had left academia to work for Dr. Miller and NASA at the first news of the comet, impressing them with his experimental work in astrobiology. Apparently, as a child he had been obsessed with a coming apocalypse, and used to fantasize about zombies and what he would do in a zombie apocalypse. It was fitting that now he was working on the stabilization of the United States in a post-comet world. Oddly, the comet's coming seemed to disappoint him only because that meant the apocalypse would not include zombies.

Suri would head the operations with Dr. Ivanov on the ground with regard to the other two comets, which would hit Earth in approximately four months' time. It was a losing fight, Suri knew. The United States did not have the means to fight two more comets. They had expended almost all of their resources in fighting Shiva, and when she fragmented and a piece of her landed on the Eurasian Plate, most of the U.S.'s remaining resources had been destroyed. Even though there were still perhaps a hundred or so IMPs, Cape

Canaveral was in ruins. She had been the only one to calculate that the comet would fragment, but the news came too late to do much about it. Now that the dust was settling on the Earth, it looked like the United States would not be able to help as much as they did beforehand.

Suri was, however, already working on modeling the IMP launches toward the comets and sending the models to Dr. Rhodes, who implemented them. The comets were currently spiraling around each other and moving in Earth's orbit in opposite directions. They danced around each other, like a musical doomsday clock, and each day that passed meant they were one day closer to colliding with Earth.

The U.S. had no infrastructure, and now they were tied to the help of the dictatorial and repressive nation of North Korea. The massive uncertainty of the future scared Suri. She first got interested in science because there was always a right answer—and there was very little uncertainty. Simply put, the industrialized human race had never dealt with an extinction-level event before, and it always happened different in the movies. There was always a happy ending in the movies.

Just then Robert walked into Suri's room. "You're ready to take my job, then?" he asked.

Suri looked up from her computer calculations, smiling and replying, "Yes, I am. We were basically running things together before my accident anyway. Heck, it might even be easier now that I don't have to check with you!"

Robert laughed. "If you make a mistake, though, you don't have someone else to blame it on . . . "

"Yes, that's true," Suri acknowledged. "So what's up?"

"Let's just go over exactly what we know now."

Suri switched around a few windows on her screen and opened up the most recent models of the comet's path toward Earth.

"Well, Comets 2 and 3 are relatively close to the Sun . . . which is helping us a lot. The outgassing is even greater since there is more surface area for the

Sun to sublimate. The two comets are moving in a helix shape through space around the Sun. In one hundred twenty-four days, our paths should meet again. At this time, I guess we have to hope that North Korea has enough power to move the comets out of the way. Because as of now, the Vishnu Spacecraft and the IMPs still traveling toward Comet 2 do not have enough force on their own to effectively move the comet out of our orbit. There might also be a way to do this with nonnuclear weapons as well, but nuclear is much more efficient."

Dr. Miller nodded, jotting things down in his notebook. He had with him a small water bottle, with the home-brewed vodka that Dr. Ivanov showed him. He told himself that he would quit as soon as the world was saved. *If* it was saved.

"We need another plan," Suri said, bringing him out of his thoughts.

"North Korea will help us defeat the comet. We'll build new IMPs and get over the critical force required to save Earth. I know it."

"Dr. Miller?"

"Yes?"

"I wanted to ask you something else, too."

"What is it, Suri?" Dr. Miller didn't look up from his notebook.

"Do . . . do you think that we were well off before the comet? Before we knew about Shiva? Do you think that humanity was flourishing, or was it on a path to destruction?"

Robert gave her a puzzled look.

"I have been thinking about the world before Shiva, and I can't shake the feeling that maybe we do need a restart, like what those rich billionaires had in mind. Global warming has been killing the planet, there is widespread corruption in politics, and global poverty looks more abundant than ever before. I guess I'm wondering if maybe the comet hitting the Earth really will be a wake-up call. *If*—and this is a big if—we save the world, what makes you think that it won't just go back to the way things were?"

Robert pulled his pen from his notebook and put

a cap on it, then looked up at Suri. He considered, and smiled warmly, before speaking. "To tell you the truth, Suri, I have no idea. It's hard I know, to think that we might just go back to doing exactly what we did before. In only two hundred years we've managed to almost destroy a planet that has supported human life for over two hundred thousand years. Now we are faced with stopping the destruction of the planet from a random comet. But if we were not here—if we had not industrialized to the point of almost destroying our planet—we would never have been able to even fragment the comet this much, and give ourselves this extra year. I know it's difficult, Suri, but let's try to focus on saving the world. Once we do that, we can start to worry about how to make sure we don't repeat the mistakes of the past two hundred years."

With that, Robert leaned in and gave Suri a kiss on the forehead. Unable to stop herself, Suri stood and hugged Dr. Miller. It felt neither awkward nor inappropriate; only needed. Suri felt forever bonded with Robert, and saying goodbye wasn't easy. Robert, too, missed that human touch. They both felt so far away from their families, and Suri sometimes felt like a daughter to him. It struck him that sometimes it was necessary to remember what he was saving the world for, and it was exactly this—this human connection. He broke away from Suri and left her office, more determined than ever to save the world.

• • •

Aboard the Ark, Janice tried to spend as much time as she could in the artificial gravity wings of the ship to make sure her muscles and health did not deteriorate. She also tried to keep herself as far away from her father as she could. She had begun working on a secret project. She was going to catalog and map every single one of the billionaire's checkpoints. The idea had come to her when she watched Alex programming. What if she were to be able to gain access to his data? If she could find a way to share it with the comet survivors on Earth, lives would be saved. So, yesterday, she memorized Alex's password when he logged in.

"Good morning," he said as he strapped into his chair.

"Morning," she replied, trying to act casual.

"It's weird not having real days and nights anymore, you know?" he asked as his computer whirred to life. "Sure, we have the 'light and dark hours' to imitate days passing, but in reality our days and nights are made up . . . "

Alex continued his musings, but Janice wasn't listening. Out of the corner of her eye, Janice watched his fingers and swift keystrokes. *Rostov1211,* she thought and memorized, *username AChekhov87.*

It was that simple!

Janice's plan was not complicated: label and map all of the checkpoints and send the information to anyone on Earth that could still use them. It seemed that Janice had found a good job for herself after all—spy. This time, however, she was doing the right thing, she was sure of it. She wondered if there were any other people on the Ark who thought the same way as her, and the first person that came to mind was Alex. Still, she couldn't be sure she could trust him, so for the present moment she decided she would go at it alone.

Her mission also had the benefit of preventing Janice from going crazy on the Ark. Every day she ate the same food, worked the same job, did the same exercises, and saw the same people. The monotony was harrowing. It was an odd sensation to be on the Ark all the time. Although the Ark's artificial gravity mimicked Earth's gravity almost exactly, something did not feel quite right about it.

Janice thought about what would happen if she got caught sending checkpoint coordinates to Earth. It would probably mean she would be imprisoned, but knowing the ruthlessness of some of the people on board, it might be worse. Aside from the billionaire businessmen, there were also rich terrorists and dictators who paid for their seats aboard the Ark. Raymond Kaser cared only if you had the money for a seat, or if he thought you'd make a good addition to his New World.

She still had to figure out how to send the information to the people on Earth—and decide whom to send it to. She quickly thought about Jeremy, though contacting him would be nearly impossible. *Think, Janice!* she thought while watching the damaged Earth pass below.

● ● ●

Karina looked over at Dustin, who was playing with his new friend Ben. He had made a rudimentary soccer ball for the kid out of a few T-shirts he had tied together and they kicked it back and forth. Since Dustin was not a soccer player, little Ben ran around him with the ball as Dustin tried to steal it from him. She watched the duo fondly as they ran around the dusty bunker, making the best out of a bad situation.

Karina was doing better as well. Their time underground was almost done, as the Israeli soldier had told them some time ago (by shouting an update in heavily accented English during their mealtime), which had its positives and negatives in Karina's mind. On the one hand, the stability of a refugee's life was comforting. They no longer worried about their meals, or thieves, or any of the aftereffects of the comet's impact. It was a boring life, but at least they had two meals a day, and a (albeit very thick and large) roof over their heads. Karina worried this would no longer be the case if they decided to go north to that island, Svalbard, which she knew Dustin wanted. They didn't really have a choice, as the angry Israeli officer said, because once the outside was deemed "hospitable," without a temperature-controlled suit or gasmask, non-Israeli citizens were told they would be evacuated from the premises.

Contrary to Karina, Dustin was incredibly excited to leave. It would mean a return to the road and an end to the monotony of being told when to eat and when to sleep. For the past month he had been a chicken in a cage, being fattened up for the inevitable plucking and decapitation. In a few days' time, however, he would go north, and hopefully Karina would join him. They had been together so long that it seemed obvious that she would go with him, but she was her own person, too. However, they didn't seem to have many options. To Dustin, it seemed the Global Seed Vault was a great choice. A great starvation was about to occur, and Dustin wanted to be prepared and ready.

9

THE THUMP GUN

August 14, 2018
Major Winter's Mansion, Texas

Jeremy and Anna looked through the door to the outside. Jeremy looked over to Anna, and her cheeks glowed radiantly under a large wide-brimmed hat. *I have the most beautiful girlfriend,* Jeremy thought dreamily.

"You ready?" Jeremy asked.

"Let's do it," Anna responded resolutely.

They were dressed head to toe in several layers of clothing, which protected their skin from the harmful UV rays. Major Winter had told them it was possible the impact could have harmed the ozone layer, the protective layer around the Earth which kept harmful ultraviolet rays from reaching the surface. Jeremy held Anna's hand just inside the foyer to the front porch of the mansion, and together they walked into their new world.

The air felt thick with humidity and had a new, unhealthy taste to it. Jeremy shielded his eyes to look at the horizon. What was once a thick forest was now a desolate apocalyptic landscape. The superheated atmosphere had burned off most of the trees' branches, making them look like huge pointed spears jutting out of the earth. The air was thick with particulate and made the horizon hazy. The ground was dirty. Even the cement road was covered with an inch of fine dirt. Jeremy swiped his finger through a line of dirt on the mansion's outside wall and saw that the paint underneath it had melted off of the brick.

"Wow," Anna said, "is that part of the comet?"

"Probably not," Jeremy answered, looking at the gunk on his finger. "Probably it's dirt from the bottom of the ocean, since that's where the comet hit."

"Wow," Anna said again, her eyes wide.

They stood silently looking at the desolate landscape.

"Want to go for a walk? It's been a while since we've been out in the Sun," she asked.

Jeremy replied by grabbing her hand and setting off, walking south.

"It's amazing that it's so hard to see," Anna remarked.

Jeremy nodded uneasily as they walked, trudging across the dirty ground. It had rained once since they had gone underground, which had caused the ground to turn into a thick muck, capable of trapping shoes. Now, a month later, the muck had dried and had turned to a misty dust, crunching noisily under their feet. After twenty minutes or so, they came to Interstate 45 and began walking south.

They were perhaps one hundred miles inland of Galveston and the Gulf of Mexico. Jeremy thought about the *Fallout* video game series, imagining that he was one of the main characters, and thought that this might be wrong way to walk. Buildings were completely destroyed, as if a tornado had swept through the landscape. There were broken-down cars, all covered with cracking mud from the debris and the subsequent rain. Jeremy looked inside one of the cars and saw a body decaying in the driver's seat.

As they walked down the interstate, Jeremy picked up on an increasingly foul odor. Anna held her nose with her fingers and scrunched up her face. Further down the road they spotted what looked like fish remains on the ground. There were dozens of fish—or what was left of them—on the ground, as well as the carcasses of birds, small animals—probably rodents—and one much larger animal, likely a deer, or maybe a small horse.

"The tsunami must have come this far and then receded," Jeremy said, thinking about the fish.

"I can't believe it," Anna said.

"Well, we are pretty far inland."

"I guess you're right. It's completely flat. There's nothing to block the water. But geez, Jer, can you even imagine it?"

He looked at her and shook his head. *I'm not sure I want to*, he thought with a shudder.

They stared solemnly at the repulsively stinky scene. Finally, they turned around and started to walk back. It was dark, and the hazy air did not help. They spoke little on the walk back.

When they approached the mansion and walked inside it, Major Winter stood with several men, loading ammunition into their weapons and putting on bulletproof vests, as if getting ready for battle.

"What's going on?" Jeremy asked, frightened.

Major Winter, who was loading a clip into an M16 assault rifle, motioned for Jeremy to come over. He walked Jeremy up the spiral staircase and toward one of the windows in front of which stood a small child's telescope. The window was blown out by severe winds—secondary climate effects of the comet. Jeremy looked into the toy telescope and saw what had caused Major Winter to tool up his militia. A small plume of smoke spiraled upward from a campsite around five miles away. In front of the smoke plume, just at the crest of the horizon, four murky figures appeared to be moving toward the mansion. Jeremy could see they were on foot, and they did not look like they were coming as friends.

"You see that small object in between the two figures in the middle?"

Jeremy nodded.

"That's what we in the industry call a 'thump gun.' You probably know it as a grenade launcher, and this one they got is a big one. They may have ripped it off a Humvee, or found it in an armory. Either way, it's no white flag."

Jeremy nodded. Anna, who had followed them, looked through the telescope.

"If they get that gun set up," she began, "could it destroy the whole mansion?"

"If they have enough grenades, definitely. That's why we are going to make sure they *don't* get that gun set up."

Major Winter handed the gun he had loaded to Jeremy.

"What? No way," Anna exclaimed, protesting.

Major Winter made no motion to argue. "Be out in ten minutes," Major Winter said to Jeremy, nodding to Anna and walking back down the stairs.

"You're not going out there," Anna said sternly to Jeremy.

Jeremy thought for a moment. He did not *want* to in the same way that Anna did not want him to, but he knew he *had* to.

"I don't see how I can refuse, Anna. Major Winter has protected us. He's allowed us to eat and to sleep, and without him who knows what would have happened? And those guys out there, with the grenade launcher, are clearly up to no good. They do not want peace. I've been training with the major for a month, so I know what I'm doing."

"You think knowing how to load or unload an assault rifle is the same as killing a real person? You have no idea what you're getting yourself into here, Jeremy. You may have supported Ian Hosmer's execution, but pulling the trigger is a lot different."

Jeremy sighed, knowing that Anna was right. The problem was that Major Winter was right, too, and he knew he had to earn his keep.

"I have to do this," he said softly.

Anna said nothing, but instead walked away, wiping away a tear from her face.

Jeremy tried not to feel guilty, and walked downstairs to put on his own bulletproof vest.

• • •

Suri was in the cafeteria, drinking coffee, and discussing the current bombardment strategy of the remaining two comets with Gerald Jan. Comet 2 was due to collide with Earth in less than four months. They had two primary weapons—Vishnu and its nuclear weapons, as well as the unknown power of the North Korean base.

The reason they couldn't predict exactly how the comets behaved was because of the sublimation jets—the pockets of gas that ejected from the comets as their outer shells slowly changed form. They would try to use the known areas of weakness in the shell to their advantage; more data on the comet was becoming available by the minute.

"As of now, the Vishnu spacecraft does not have the power to move Comet 2 significantly out of the way. But combined with the IMPs, and if North Korea can build and launch some of their own IMPs, we might be able to stop it. That is a big 'might,' though."

"How is our eye in the sky?" Suri asked. "How is Dr. Rhodes doing?"

"Nia is fine. She actually just woke up, and should be online shortly," Gerald answered.

Since communications had come back online, Nia Rhodes could communicate via a webcam. Within a few minutes her face appeared on the screen, and Dr. Rhodes looked out at them, showing a dark sky behind her.

"Hello! Do you copy, Los Alamos?"

"Copy, Nia. You're online."

Dr. Nia Rhodes looked strung out. Suri had expected to see a woman with a long face, and dark skin, with jet-black hair and olive eyes. She expected to see stark, angled features and a wry smile, like the one in the military photo, which was her webcam icon. However, the Nia who had been in space for over a year looked radically different. She had cut her hair so it was short and stylish. Her eyes had deep bags under them and Suri could see Nia's cheekbones jut out of her face, making her look gaunt.

"Roger that. All systems go here, Gerald. From the preliminary data, it looks like Comet 2, at twenty kilometers in diameter, is not moving significantly out of Earth's orbit," Nia said reluctantly.

Suri's heart sank, and Gerald replied with a despondent sigh.

"That's three times the power we have on the ship," Gerald said, regaining his composure and thinking hard. "We knew something like this could happen, and to fill you in, Doctor, we have some bit of good news. Dr. Robert Miller is joining a team in east Asia, a team that supposedly has a working launch station and an abundant arsenal of missiles."

Dr. Rhodes, who had been in the U.S. Air Force before being employed by Gerald Jan in this new position, had narrowed her eyes. She already knew what "east Asian" nation he meant, but had to ask anyway.

"You mean to tell me that we are going to trust North Korea?"

At this, Suri cut in. "If you know of another country that has a working launch station we would love to go that route, but as it stands we must give North Korea a try."

"You're Suri Lahdka, right?" Nia asked, momentarily forgetting about the daunting task ahead. She had only read about Suri in the news and heard about her on the radio, and was surprised to find out she was so young.

"Yes, that's me. It's nice to meet you."

"Nice to see we have some females here, right? We need to keep these guys in check; make sure they don't try anything too crazy, am I right?"

Suri laughed and nodded before replying, "There's no other option than to trust North Korea, Dr. Rhodes. If it makes you feel better, don't think of it as trusting North Korea. Instead, think of it as trusting that humanity, no matter the cost, will sacrifice everything in order to survive."

You don't know the half of it, Nia thought. *Here I am telling Gerald that the spaceship I'm on has a futile mission. What am I doing up here . . . ?*

"So, North Korea will be online in around two months, and Robert is en route there now," Suri continued, "so, we three have a decision to make. I have discussed this with Dr. Miller as well and I think we have a good plan for how to divert the comets. At the moment, the helical pattern of movement of the comets means that it would be advantageous to blast each comet near its surface as we did before with the fractured body. I believe this will allow us the maximum thrust from the jets. The sublimation jets are focused near the equator of Comet 2. The helical orbital shape is also helpful. We will aim to detonate each nuclear warhead in between the comets, so that the blast meant for one comet will also move the other comet in the opposite direction. We will aim to move each comet farther away from the other, and hopefully move one or both outside our orbit. I've sent you the data on the modeling for the IMPs under your control now."

Right, Nia remembered. *Now I have to control the IMPs as well because they don't have communications with them anymore.*

"Gravity is keeping these two comets in that helical orbit, right? With their center of mass somewhere in between them?" Nia asked.

"Yes, that's right," Gerald answered.

"Well, won't gravity be working against us then, since the comets will want to go back into that helical orbit?" Nia asked.

"Yes, it will. But gravity is pretty much against us at all times at this point. And this way we maximize the nuclear blasts that we have left," Suri said.

"Got it."

"So," Suri continued, "we also have communications back online with several other nations, all who have promised all their available resources to help us. It's not much, but we are a global fight against the next attack."

Nia used the break in Suri's update to ask a question not related to the comets: "What about this ship orbiting Earth? The large one? It launched around the same time the Vishnu spacecraft did. What is it?"

Suri looked over at Gerald, who she thought could better answer this question. She knew about the Ark, but not much. Gerald had actually been asked to be on it.

"Well, I know you've been training and haven't had too much time to check out the news, but the rumors about the ship being built by the billionaire class? Well, their ship is real. They've aptly called it the Ark, though they didn't take two of every species. Instead, a few choice animals that can feed people, like cows and chickens, and millions of seeds which also will be able to feed people, were stowed on board. And of course, the billionaires who paid for the construction were also allowed on.

"We should be wary of it, though. I have tried to make contact with their ship many times to make sure they aren't going to try to sabotage plans to save Earth again—"

"Wait," Nia exclaimed, "what do you mean *again*?"

Suri cut in and explained to Nia that the attack on her—the attack that had almost killed her and destroyed Miami—was the work of a group under the control of the billionaire elite. "The billionaire elite believe that the reduction in the population will be beneficial for Earth, so they tried to stop us from doing our work."

Jesus Christ, Nia thought. "Do you think they have a plan to sabotage our strategies to divert the comet a second time?" Nia asked.

"I don't think so. I'm hoping they think the first comet impact was enough for them. Our human population will certainly be heavily depleted from the impact. Especially from starvation. But I could be wrong—they could be planning something. That's why I have been trying to contact them. We must be ready to stop them from committing another act of terrorism."

They concluded their talk. One positive part of their current plan was how much accurate data they received from the Vishnu Spacecraft. With it they could measure the comets' structural composition, sublimation rate, orbital path, and many other variables with extreme accuracy.

Suri hustled through the hallways to the other side of the complex so she could talk to Robert one last time before he left. Her legs were moving better every day, even though her skin itched from the skin grafts that she had needed.

The airfield was on the opposite side of the complex; a long walk and a short elevator ride to one of three Air Force One jets. President Chaplin had allowed Robert to borrow one of her planes and a team of Marines and pilots to get to the Korean Peninsula— thankfully nixing the plan for a boat. When Suri arrived, Robert greeted her with a nod, and she smiled at her best friend and closest ally.

"It seems like I just got back to work, and we aren't going to be side by side anymore."

"You know one of us has to stay here to run things."

"Yes," Suri replied, and filled Robert in on the conversation with Nia Rhodes and Gerald.

"Sounds like a plan. I will phone you when I touch down in North Korea, but I think this is a good plan. Hopefully the plan will go well, and then we can finally put this whole comet business to rest."

"If we do, the world will be a different place when we are done."

Robert put a hand on Suri's shoulder. "It already is, Suri. Even though things look bleak with the size of our arsenal and the size of Comet 2, we have to try." Robert leaned over and hugged Suri so tightly she coughed a little. "We have to try."

Suri felt a few tears coming to her eyes. *Things do look pretty hopeless*, she thought.

Robert turned then and walked up the staircase into the modified Boeing 747. He was probably the first non-president of the United States to be the principle passenger on the plane. He brought with him a duffel filled with clothes. Despite his lack of care for his appearance, he did not want to be forced to wear one of those dictatorial smocks he saw Kim Ha Lee wear on the news. He also brought with him another suitcase filled with computers and documents about the most recent data concerning the comets.

Robert gave his bags to one of the security guards, who lugged it up the staircase. Once on the stairway, Robert saw Suri waving at him. He waved back at her, hoping he would see her again, and walked up. Once he got into the plane, he sighed. A sign saying "Presidential Office" was posted at the base of a second staircase. *I'm getting too old for this*, Robert thought, thinking about this new adventure, feeling his heart rate increase and his breathing quicken.

He stopped by the cockpit. Robert poked his head in the door.

"We have to make a stop before Korea."

The pilot looked back at Robert, who nodded while flipping some switches in the cockpit.

"You got it, boss."

10

ENEMIES

August 15, 2018
Major Winter's Mansion, Texas

Major Winter told Jeremy everything he needed to do. The major also gave him one of the easier jobs, as he knew he would be less prepared in a possible war zone than those who had already seen it. Jeremy sat in the downstairs room on the far west side of the mansion. There were men stationed at all the windows, and Jeremy was equipped with a close-range machine gun. They did not have any sniper rifles, unfortunately, otherwise this job would be very easy indeed and Jeremy would probably not even have an assignment. As it stood, he was tasked with shooting the men if they came within range.

"What exactly does 'within range' mean?" Jeremy had asked the major.

"If you hear us shooting, that's your cue. Don't shoot beforehand, and stay out of sight."

"Got it."

Major Winter then told him three things on his first mission holding a weapon.

"First, be quiet."

Jeremy nodded.

"Second, as I said before, no shooting until one of us fires first. Once the shooting begins, everyone starts shooting."

Jeremy nodded.

"Third, about the door downstairs to the others: make sure it stays shut. Do not let anyone open it for any reason, even to check on us. As far as we know, these attackers do not know there is a 'downstairs.' So, if they are just here to pillage and by some disaster we all die trying to save this place, at least our friends down below will still be safe."

Jeremy nodded a third time.

Jeremy sat, waiting nervously, his palms sweating against the metal hilt of his machine gun. It was heavy. He looked out at the hazy field in front of him. The figures were still shrouded and invisible. Jeremy felt hyperaware, like he had taken some of Dustin's ADHD pills. His heart beat fast and he constantly moved his eyes, scanning the field in front of him. He wore a military helmet and body armor and two extra cartridges of ammunition. He didn't remember how many bullets were in a cartridge, and this suddenly seemed incredibly important. He desperately wanted to pull the trigger and make sure the gun worked but Major Winter had warned him to remain quiet.

"We have the element of surprise since they do not know that we know they are coming. You have to trust your gun will fire." Major Winter then repeated the Rifleman's Creed, which Jeremy had always thought was just a part of the movie *Full Metal Jacket*.

I have to trust my gun, Jeremy thought, before reciting the words of the movie to himself: "This is my rifle. There are many like it but this one is mine."

Jeremy heard the front door open quietly, and a few men hustled out of it. They flanked the front field, moving far to the left and right. Major Winter had told him their strategy when he was getting ready. Getting ready meant putting on heavy pieces of Kevlar that were supposed to be able to stop a bullet from shredding his insides.

"We are going to surround the enemy. It is risky to leave the relative safety of the mansion, but in this case it is more than worth our strategic position given our number of men. A quick test for you, why else would we want to flank these attackers?"

Jeremy had thought for a moment before answering. After a few seconds he ventured a guess: "To see if there are any more? If these men are maybe a diversion? It also means we can get them before they have time to set up the thump gun."

Major Winter smiled, replying, "Exactly. Now, I'll be in the room right above you, and I'll be in communication with 'Alpha,' our name for the team on the ground going west. The team going east, is 'Beta.'

We are 'Base.' This stuff shouldn't be important at the moment, but I just wanted to let you know."

"Got it," Jeremy had said, nervously. This is when his palms had begun to sweat, and he asked, "The others are going to be alright, right? I mean, they are underground, so even if the mansion does get hit, they will be okay?"

"Do your job, and everyone down there will be safe."

Everyone down there, Jeremy thought, echoing Major Winter's words. *Anna.*

He repeated those words to himself as he stared out into the haze. *I wonder how long it's going to look so hazy?* he thought. Jeremy held the heavy weapon so the barrel was resting on the window, and he waited. It turned out that the waiting caused him much more anxiety than he anticipated. Every single shimmer and movement in the distance, even the slightest drift or shift that caught his eye made his muscles tense.

Then, after what seemed like ages, Jeremy saw the figures hustling toward them. The two in the middle were still holding the large grenade launcher. There were six total figures, and they were all wearing large ski goggles, and baseball caps. They all had long shirts as well, but those were torn in several places. They looked like they had come out of a *Mad Max* movie. Jeremy looked left and right and noticed Major Winter's men hiding behind some blackened tree stumps, waiting. The men continued walking toward the mansion, and then the enemies lowered the thump gun to the ground and began to set it up.

Jeremy held his breath watching. He did not have to wait long, however, because immediately the Alpha and Beta teams began shooting at the assailants.

"That's my cue," Jeremy gasped, trying to train his gun on the group.

He thought they were too far to hit but aimed at them and put his finger on the trigger. Then he pulled it as the cracks of gunfire rang through the air and bullet casings flew out of his rifle. He saw two of the Alpha team members fall down in a clump.

All the enemies fell to the ground, and the grenade

launcher, looking more like some kind of antiaircraft or antitank weapon, sat unharmed and unused on the battlefield. Its barrel slowly swung to one side, causing the weapon to tilt slightly.

I wonder if it was one of my bullets, Jeremy thought, looking at the sad pile of bodies in the distance. Everything had happened so fast it almost seemed anticlimactic. They had lost two of their own men. Jeremy's radio crackled to life, and he heard Major Winter telling everyone to return to Base.

Two of the militiamen picked up the grenade launcher, hustling it back to the mansion. Jeremy could hear them all piling into the main room, and Major Winter barking orders at them all.

"Everyone to a window. We will wait to make sure no one else is coming."

So they waited. Jeremy tried to breathe slowly in and out but his heart still leapt out of his chest with every beat. He hoped he'd hit one of the men he was aiming for but it was hard to tell for sure. At first he was proud, seeing one of the men slump to the side when he'd shot him. *Or was it someone else and I just shot at the ground?* he thought to himself. He couldn't decide what was worse, hitting the attacker he thought he'd hit, or not hitting him.

When the half hour was up, Major Winter ordered six men to check the bodies and bring them back to the back of the mansion.

"Scott, Travis, and Tiny first," the major added.

Jeremy volunteered to go. He wasn't sure why. He slung the gun over his shoulder, letting the muzzle point to the ground. The gun dug into his back. He walked out to the bodies, which really weren't as far away as he'd thought in the haze. He tried not to look at the blood. It stained the hard ground.

He dragged one of the dead Alpha team members back towards the mansion. Then he went back for the enemies. He tried to pick one of them up, a big man who must have weighed just under two hundred pounds, but it was impossible. He had never carried a dead body before, but now he felt like he knew what the expression "dead weight" truly meant. He had to drag the body, and by the time he finished his back ached and sweat dripped off his nose.

Then the major told everyone to get a shovel out of the back room of the mansion, and start digging.

"Seven graves, six feet down and six feet across. And wide enough. Two there for our men, and five down the road."

Jeremy began to dig and it took him a while to finish his hole. When he did finish, the sweat was pouring down his face and his back. Then he grabbed one of the bodies by the shoulders to move to his hole, and noticed that the goggles had come off the man. It was the same one he had aimed at during the firing—this man had been the one standing to the left of the grenade launcher. He could tell by the odd mix of clothing he had on: tight long sleeve Under Armour and a plain golf shirt. Jeremy made the mistake of looking down; the disfigured face of agony stared back at him, through eternally dark, crimson eyes.

11

MAKING MOVES

Later That Day
Major Winter's Mansion, Texas

Anna fidgeted nervously in her room, thinking the policy of keeping the women safely away from the battle was a bit antiquated, but in this case it gave her a little more time to think, and to think without Jeremy there. She thought she was pregnant. At least, she was pretty sure—she didn't exactly have access to a test, but there were signs.

The woman Anna worked with on the garden, Tabatha, was a nurse before the comet hit. Before going underground, she "liberated" as many medications as she could get her hands on and called her son, Marcus, who was living with an old friend named

Major Winter. It turned out Marcus had been trying to call to invite her to come live with him and the others in the compound, and in two hours, she'd made the trip. It was Tabatha who had suggested the cause of many of her symptoms, and when they all lined up in her head it was a glass-shattering realization.

Her period was late, but Anna had just thought that was the stress associated with living underground. Her legs felt sore, but again she thought that was due to working on her feet all day. She felt tired at all times of the day, her breasts felt sore, and she had nausea so bad she even vomited once—especially strange since she hadn't eaten anything that day. Then, when she was having lunch one day, eating the freeze-dried chicken for the seventh consecutive day, to her surprise, it tasted absolutely delicious! She then remembered reading somewhere that if a woman's taste buds started changing dramatically, it might mean she was pregnant. Still, she passed it off as if it were some kind of strange coincidence. Finally it came to her, one night when she had been sitting with Tabatha, building the support hoops for the tomatoes.

"Sounds to me like you're pregnant," Tabatha said, raising one eyebrow at Anna.

It was here that the glass shattered. "No, no, no," Anna began, "No, no, *no* . . . "

"Honey, saying *no* isn't going to make you un-pregnant."

Anna's heartbeat accelerated.

"It's not possible," she said, "I need this now? Now? Tabatha, the planet is about to explode. Do you know what kind of world I would be bringing a child in to? No, you don't. No one does. There are no doctors, no prenatal care. Definitely no hospital." She paused as a horrible thought filled her. "Oh God. And definitely no anesthesia!"

Tabatha rubbed Anna's back as she started breathing heavily and shaking her head. Then Anna began to cry.

"What am I going to do?" Anna sobbed quietly.

. . .

Robert looked through the window of the Air Force One plane at the ground below. Everything was covered in a thick haze, so that he only saw the landing strip shortly before touching down. There were fields of half-burned trees and bare fields, but Robert couldn't see much more. It was a short plane ride to Major Winter's mansion and he hadn't had time to really settle in to the flight, or get any meaningful work done. When the wheels of the plane hit the dusty landing strip of some tiny Texan airport, Robert looked toward the back of the plane's exterior as the sky filled with dust, kicked up by the landing. By the time the plane stopped dead it had kicked up a dust cloud a mile and a half long.

The back of the plane was equipped with a black SUV—the Presidential SUV. Robert found the keys to it in the desk in the office. Even the keychain had the Presidential Seal on it.

Robert told the security detail that he would go drive the fifteen minutes to Major Winter's mansion by himself. Obviously, they wouldn't have it.

"Sir, with all due respect, the President of the United States told us to protect you, so that's what we are going to do."

"Very well," Robert answered, knowing a lost cause when he saw one.

Robert walked out onto the ground to survey the land before hopping into the SUV. The ground was craggy and alien-looking. He sank into it when he stepped down and the plane's dust cloud behind him was traveling towards him. He stuck his nose in his shirt and headed back toward the car. The Marine escort followed him.

Before long the old mansion came into view, amidst the odd, spiky-looking remnants of trees. He hoped to find his old friend, Major Anton Winter. Jeremy would probably be there, too. *He could be a help to me in Los Alamos,* Robert thought.

Robert's SUV caused a dust upheaval similar to

the plane, though on a smaller magnitude. By the time Robert walked from the car to the house, he was entirely covered in a thin film of dust.

After trying to get as much of the dirt off of his face as he could, Robert knocked. He knocked on the door as loud as he could, and waved into the camera.

"Hello!" Robert yelled, thinking that Major Winter and anyone else in the mansion would be far underground at the time. Imagine his surprise when he found the door open quickly, but only wide enough for the barrel of a machine gun to poke itself through. It struck Robert just below the sternum.

"Whoa, whoa, I'm unarmed. I'm a friend of Major Anton Winter. My name is Robert Miller."

The gun didn't move. It sat against Robert's chest for another few agonizing seconds, and then it quickly withdrew into the house and the door closed. Some bolts were shifted around, and the door finally opened.

"Sorry about that, Robert. I wasn't expecting you—I was expecting . . . someone else. Come inside,"

Major Winter said wearily, ushering him by the guard who'd presumably stuck the gun barrel in his gut.

Robert looked around. There were military men sitting all around the entrance room, somberly cleaning their weapons or looking vaguely in front of themselves. One man was shot, bleeding from the shoulder, but other than that no one seemed hurt.

"What happened here?" Robert asked.

Major Winter led him into the room that used to be the restaurant. There was no "weapons check" anymore. They sat opposite each other and Major Winter walked him through the last two months of life at the mansion, and explained to him quickly why his men looked so somber.

Robert told him he was sorry to hear it.

"They'll be fine. The kid, though, Jeremy, he seems a little shook up about it all."

"I need to ask you something, Anton," Robert said, looking up at the major.

"What can I do for you, Robert?"

Robert explained he was going to North Korea in

an effort to use their weapons systems to help defeat the comet.

"I want you to come with me and act as my security. I need someone I can trust completely over there, and I don't know any of the guys with me now. Will you come?"

Major Winter considered the offer, thinking.

"There are a lot of things I'm in charge of here, Rob. I have to make sure everyone gets fed, for one."

Robert nodded, understandingly.

"Anton, I need your help. If I don't make sure that the comet is stopped, we might not make it out of this year alive. And by *we* I mean everyone who is left on Earth."

Major Winter thought for another minute, rubbing the stubble on his chin. Then he nodded his head. They shook hands and Major Winter said he needed five minutes to get ready.

"Oh," he asked, still putting on his jacket. "How are we leaving?"

"By plane."

Major Winter screwed his face into an *I'm-impressed* expression.

"Is Jeremy here? I'd like to talk to him."

"He's in the main room," Major Winter answered. "I'll give you a second, and I'll be out front."

Robert nodded and sat thinking about everything Major Winter had told him, about life in the compound after the comet had hit. When he looked around, he didn't recognize any of the soldiers as Jeremy. He asked one of the nearest ones for help.

"He's downstairs," he said, pointing down a stairway.

"Thank you."

Robert followed the man's instructions and headed down the small staircase, ducking to make sure he didn't hit his head on the low ceiling. He stepped into a dungeon-like hallway, and found Jeremy sitting on the ground in the dark, the hallway lit only by a small construction light halfway down the hall.

"Jeremy, hi!" Robert said, surprised at his own excitement at seeing the boy. To Robert, Jeremy almost looked like a different person. He was bigger, more muscular, and had the makings of a respectable beard.

"Robert?" Jeremy looked up, surprised and baffled at seeing the familiar face. "What are you doing here? Where did you come from?" Jeremy scrambled to his feet and shook hands with the scientist.

"I'm sort of on a mission." Robert paused, and upon seeing Jeremy's grim countenance he added, "Are you doing alright?"

"Yeah, sure," Jeremy answered. "I'm doing fine. Just a . . . chaotic day."

"Yeah, Major Winter told me," Robert said, sitting down on the floor next to Jeremy.

Robert then explained about North Korea and what he was doing.

"Listen," Robert said when he'd finished, "you're a smart kid, and you've proven yourself. Maybe more importantly, I feel like I can trust you."

Jeremy didn't know what to say. For a moment he

had wondered if Robert was going to invite him to North Korea. But the moment had passed.

"If you ever need a place to go," Robert began, "and you can make it to Los Alamos, I could use you over there in some capacity, I'm sure of it. Suri Lahdka, who you met, will certainly have a job for you. I'll be in touch with her over the next couple of months. I also spoke with Secretary Brighton about you."

"The Secretary of State?" Jeremy asked quickly.

"Yes."

"You came here to take Major Winter to be your protection, right?" Jeremy asked.

"That's right," Robert answered.

"Thank you, Dr. Miller," Jeremy said. "I appreciate you looking out for me." Jeremy didn't know what else to say.

"Well, I do wish you good luck, Jeremy. And I wish I could see you for a little longer and catch up, but it's time for me to get back to work." Then they nodded at each other, and Jeremy could have sworn he saw Robert shed a small tear.

"I understand, Dr. Miller," Jeremy said, smiling. "Good luck!"

"Thank you."

They shook hands, and Robert walked back up the stairs and found Major Winter talking to his men in the main room of the mansion.

"Let's do it," Robert said.

"I'll just speak with my men here, and meet you in the car."

Robert nodded and walked out to give Major Winter some privacy with his troops. He stepped over a curious red stain in the dusty ground before he unlocked the car and got in. As he turned the ignition, he thought about Jeremy. *He got so much older,* Robert thought. *I guess he's not a kid anymore . . . he looks like a man.*

Robert wished he could have taken Jeremy with him to North Korea, but it was too dangerous. He didn't know what the mission would bring, and didn't want to have to look after another person while he worked.

Major Winter exited the mansion, carrying a heavy bag on his shoulder. They drove back to the airplane without speaking, until Major Winter saw the plane.

"You didn't tell me the plane you had is Air Force One, Robert! I've never been on one of those before. I thought it was going to be a military plane, but *Air Force One*! You've really moved up in the world," the major joked.

• • •

"So, should we walk north?" Dustin asked, extending his arm to Karina for her to hold. It was the last day they could stay in the Israeli bunker before being forced to leave. The elevator was broken, so they had to take the stairs up to the ground. Dustin had hoped that Ben's family might offer to help them, but they hadn't, and so here they were, on their own.

Karina grabbed Dustin's hand, thinking she didn't have a better idea.

"We have to pick a direction, so we might as well go towards your seed vault," she answered.

They were covered head to toe in clothing to protect themselves from the Sun. Dustin looked out at the dusty road. It looked abysmal and apocalyptic, covered by muck from the Earth's crust—it had rained the day before. The bunker was on the northern outskirts of Tel Aviv, so behind them they could see the dilapidated city. Windows were mostly blown out of their panes by some extreme weather event they had escaped. In fact, many of the buildings were half-standing—they looked like they'd been struck by a tornado.

To the west, the sea level had risen significantly. They noticed tiny waves lapping against the elevated freeway.

"The ice caps must have melted," Karina reasoned.

Dustin nodded. "That does make sense."

On the freeway—where they now stood—the rain

had caused the dust to turn into a thick grimy stew, which stuck to their shoes like quicksand; every step became harder than the one they took before it, and their bags seemed heavier. The mud was getting everywhere. They walked along for a few more hours before Karina spoke up.

"Dustin, everything is covered in this mud. How are we going to sleep? We can't even lay down here."

Dustin looked back at Karina, who was walking a few paces behind him. Behind her, Dustin could barely see the haze of Tel Aviv anymore, even though they were only a few miles away from the city. The haze gave everything a colorless hue, a sort of old-style sepia that depressed the senses.

"I don't know, maybe in a building?" But as he said this he looked around at the crumbling remains of what was once a Tel Aviv suburb and realized this would not be a smart idea either.

"Dustin, we can't do this," Karina said despondently.

"Karina what else are we supposed to do? We can't go back either," Dustin angrily answered.

They stood there together huffing and puffing, and looking generally tired. Not to mention they were both emaciated from eating little other than the caloric necessities for at least three months. The only food they carried with them were some meal packets supplied to them by the Israeli Army, a gift given hesitantly by the officer in charge.

They decided for a minute to sit down, but then didn't know how to even do that. If they sat down, their only jeans would get completely full of mud, and if they sat down on their backpacks those would probably get even muddier than their butts. They stood, already annoyed by their lack of options.

"We should call this new place Tatooine," Dustin remarked, thinking of Luke Skywalker's home planet.

"What? Tattooing?" Karina replied, but only distantly, as she was focusing on the black SUV driving towards them. It was creating a wake of mud.

"Do you think we should get off the road?" she asked, pointing toward the SUV driving toward them.

"Yeah, I do."

They did get off the road, but only slightly, because Dustin wanted to check to see who it was.

The car slowed down once it noticed the two hitch-hikers sticking their thumbs out. It even slowed down enough so that the mud wake was small enough that it didn't cover them. The car stopped right next to them, but its blacked-out windows made it impossible to see who it was. Slowly the back window rolled down. There was a small eager-looking child smiling at both them.

"Ben!" Dustin exclaimed.

"Hi guys!" Ben replied. "Do you need a ride?"

Dustin and Karina shared a look of relief, nodded enthusiastically, and tromped to the other side of the car. Dustin sat in the middle and Karina to the right, and once they did, two begrudging parents looked back at them.

The father, who was named David, had on a black

shirt and jeans. He wore a bulletproof vest and had on a yarmulke. David looked down disapprovingly at the newcomers' shoes, which had tracked in around four pounds of mud on their way into the car.

"Hello, Dustin. Karina." David grunted. "Get in."

Esther, David's wife, looked back and smiled at Dustin and Karina.

Karina and Dustin looked over at little Ben. He smiled and nodded happily, but the look of disdain on David's face made it clear that he did not approve of the two Americans tagging along.

It looked like, at the very least, they would be in for an awkward ride.

12

NEW PLANS

August 15, 2018
Medium Earth Orbit, Ark Spacecraft

Janice Effran looked solemnly out of the exercise room toward the Earth she had left in favor of the big metal ship she now called home. She sat on the floor, playing with the flash drive in her hand. She tossed it up and down, catching it and twirling it around her thumb. It held the locations of all the checkpoints that the Ark billionaires had created for when they returned. She also had it stored as a file on her private profile on the Ark. Figuring out a way to send it down to Earth was difficult, and she realized if she could trust him, she could use Alex's help. Alex just might know enough programming to get the job delivered, but then—someone would need to be equipped to receive her transmissions as well.

If she did get it done, then maybe her friends that she stayed with—Jeremy, Dustin, Anna, and Karina—could use them. If by some miracle they were still alive, they could use the checkpoints to live a little longer, and maybe start to rebuild. But, it might only last them four months. She'd learned last week in a bulletin on the Ark that it was likely the Earth would be finished off by the larger of the two remaining fragments. The destruction date was less than four months away.

Apparently these billionaires have access to the comet data, Janice thought. *I wonder if they have telescopes, or if they have a mole somewhere?*

"Janice?"

Janice realized she was no longer the only person in the exercise room, and saw Alex sitting across from her.

"Oh, hi, Alex."

"Hey."

"How's it going?"

"Good enough under circumstances," Alex answered, before asking, "What's that in your hand?"

"Oh, nothing. Just a little side project I'm working on. Something to pass the time."

"Passing the time seems the hardest thing to do here," Alex replied, taking a seat next to her.

"Yeah, seriously. I set up a calendar where I can cross off the days until we get to go back to Earth."

"Wow, me too!" Alex laughed, before showing her an app he had written, showing a calendar on his phone's screen. With a finger swipe, the days of the month could be crossed off. Alex crossed one off for fun, and a bitmoji "Alex" character did a little dance on the screen, before fist-bumping the air and disappearing in a wisp of smoke. It made Janice laugh.

"That's so cute," she said.

"I thought you'd like it," Alex replied.

The light above the door to the exercise room flashed yellow three times. For the past week—after hitting the fourteen month mark of being on the Ark—a new way to eat had been instituted. It turned out that even on the Ark full of billionaires, there was a class system. The lights represented when certain classes were allowed to eat, and Janice was in the lowest of the classes. The lowest class ate when the yellow light flashed on and off three times in all common rooms signaling their food was ready. When she got up to leave, Alex grabbed her wrist, looking up at her. It took Janice aback, because Alex had never touched her before.

"Before you go, I wanted to tell you something." He let go of her wrist.

"What's going on, Alex?"

"You know my father, right?"

"I've seen him on the ship, and I know he's Russian, if that's what you mean."

"Well, he is also an expert in drilling, which is how he made his fortune. He mines for minerals and metals in Russia. He's rich, of course, but the leader of the Ark, that Raymond Kaser, he wanted my father aboard the ship because of his knowledge of drilling, not just for his share of money. I overheard my father and Kaser talking a few days ago, about the two comets. They were upset that apparently North Korea has a useable launch facility and missiles that can stop one or both comets from hitting Earth. They want to destroy the launch facility."

"God, what is with these guys? Why do they want to stop saving the world?" Janice asked angrily.

"Shh, we can't talk about this so loud. We can't be overheard. What I'm saying is that they want to hurt those people, and I . . . I want to stop them. I don't care about 'restarting the world' like they do. I just want to live, and I want as many people to live as possible. And I don't know . . . I guess I just wanted to tell someone else that I'm not like these other guys."

Janice said nothing, and then Alex continued.

"You seem trustworthy, and I don't think you're like them. I know I'm not," Alex repeated.

Janice came within seconds of telling Alex her plan with the checkpoints; it was on the tip of her tongue.

At the last second, though, she recanted, saying simply, "I'm not like them either."

Considering her past, this might not be right. *But maybe I can change things. Maybe Alex and I can change things together.* She began to hope it was true.

• • •

Dr. Nia Rhodes: Two Months, Six Days Post Impact:

The comets are rapidly decreasing in size since they are so close to the Sun. I had not expected this rate of decrease; by the time they reach the Earth they will be at half their current size! This is good news for everyone still stuck on Earth.

When I took this mission, I thought of myself as a saint, and a martyr, and I guess you don't even know why. Well, it's time for me to explain. This ship, Vishnu, was built for one thing only—to shoot nukes at rocks in space, and to keep me alive while doing it. Every single cubic millimeter of this ship was designed solely for that purpose. That means that there was very little thought as to a reentry to Earth-orbit strategy.

This is why I thought of myself as a saint, but since this is a journal, I don't know why I should continue to lie to myself. Part of me wants to be remembered. And if I am successful, I am fairly certain the name Dr. Nia Rhodes will survive longer than any living thing on the planet today. I will be a hero. A legend. Part of me looks forward to that, even though I won't be able to see it myself. At least I hope they will call me a hero, otherwise I'm sacrificing my life for nothing . . .

• • •

Robert Miller sat with Major Winter, seatbelts fastened, and chairs in their upright position as they prepared for landing. They would have put their tray tables up, but it being Air Force One, those were absent. Robert swigged down a large gulp—it was the first shot of the last bottle of Dr. Ivanov's tepid vodka. Major Winter raised an eyebrow when he saw Robert down the spirit, but said nothing. The plane's landing was smooth. It was a rainy day in North Korea as the stairway door opened.

Robert saw a battalion of North Koreans standing in the rain, awaiting them. In front stood the North Korean President, Kim Ha Lee. There were two men standing just behind him, and many military leaders standing several paces behind them. Robert figured one of those two attending men was Dr. Kang, and the other was a translator. They were all wearing the dictatorial jumpsuits Robert had seen on television. *This is really happening,* he thought in awe.

The Secret Service men that President Chaplin had given to Robert walked down first, followed by Major Winter, and finally Robert. Robert thought he was in a movie, whereas he would much rather be in a lab.

"Dr. Miller. Welcome to North Korea. I present to you the Supreme Leader Kim Ha Lee." The translator stopped and Robert felt compelled to bow. He did not do this, however, instead extending his hand.

"The Supreme Leader expects a bow," the

translator said in a slightly pleading tone. Robert, stubborn as he was, noticed that his lack of bowing could mean punishment for both himself, the others with him, and this innocent translator. *Wait,* Robert thought, *why isn't Kim Ha Lee talking? Didn't President Chaplin speak to him in English?*

Confused, he managed a small bow. The translator continued.

"My name is Mr. Yuan; we have spoken before." He indicated another man standing near him. "This is Dr. Kang, who you and I will be working with."

Robert nodded at the man, who gave a slight bow as well. Then Kim Ha Lee spoke, in a calm, even voice, with a slight French accent.

"I am very thankful for your help, and look forward to seeing the world—and our great nation, North Korea—live another year. Perhaps even many."

"Me, too," Robert replied, eager to get to work, "and thank you for calling us to help as well." He took a deep breath, trying to take it all in. "And together we will save the world."